Out of the Nest
A MAURIZIO
CHE NON SA DI ESSERE STATO
IL MIO PRIMO AMORE,
E A SETH,
CHE HA RIDEFINITO IL SIGNIFICATO
DELLA PAROLA AMORE

Second edition 2017

Cover illustration by Thomas Webb

http://www.thomas-webb-arts.com/

FOREWORD

I LEFT A FEW ITALIAN words in the text because they really cannot be translated without losing some of the flavor. I hope you will forgive the fact that most of them are swearwords. I am sure you will get a sense for their meaning within the first few chapters.

The capitalization of God reflects the views, at times changing, of the characters uttering it.

— GBA

PROLOGUE

SEPTEMBER 1990, ARESE, A SMALL town in the Milan province, Northern Italy

As I stared at his face, I understood the question he dared not ask.

He glued his gaze on me, a slight blush betraying feelings I had not suspected. We had always been friends. I had never looked at him that way, but I allowed myself to: he was so darn handsome. His wild hair made him seem like the rebel he pretended to be. Instead, he was sweet and sincere even if, on one occasion or two, he had done rather questionable deeds. Boys will be boys. I knew he could be a jerk. His mesmerizing eyes, locked on mine, held no promise of that. He interrupted my catatonic state with his question.

"Lee, do you want to be my girlfriend?"

Was it possible that the love of my life had been there all along?

PART 1

1

Do Wishes Expire?

One year earlier

Fall days stretched like a long evening. Cicadas deadened, and the creaking of dry leaves underfoot underlined a remembered silence. Summer's scents, tainted by a note of decay, lingered under the ripe light of the sun. Curtain call; life slowed for winter. The seaside turned into a melancholy echo of empty shores. The telly, even on Video Music channel, streamed ads for schoolbags, pencils, and notebooks. Middle school was imminent.

A new video invaded the screen. I sighed. I would have rather watched cartoons, but my older sister Viola detained the remote.

For once, I found myself entranced by the guy on TV. He was singing about having lost something while becoming an adult, something he couldn't put his finger on, which used to make things brighter and fuller.

"Wow, who's that?" I asked.

Viola answered, "That's *Liberi Liberi* by Vasco Rossi. He's huge. If you like him, I can hand you down a couple of cassettes."

Our strained relationship had improved either because I was older or because she was about to move out to attend college in Padua. She had quit her DJ career at Radio Arese City, but she was still the musical go-to.

I exclaimed, "Thank you! That would be awesome. You don't like him anymore?"

Viola shrugged. "Not so much. On a more interesting topic, what's with the wish bracelet, Lee?" She smirked.

"Oh, this?" I touched the red cotton thread, which had been resting around my wrist since the spring. "Nothing."

"Oh, don't you play dumb with me! Red is for love, so who's the lucky one?"

Heat rose to my cheeks, and I hated myself for it. "Well, then you know if I tell someone, my wish won't come true!"

Viola chuckled, turning her attention back to the TV.

The bracelet looked far from breaking, which meant Flavio would not ask me to be his girlfriend anytime soon. Good, since that had been more Mom's hope than mine. I had played along to fill the hole left by my parents' separation with something new and exciting, but Flavio was not it as the summer had revealed.

Worse, a worrisome heartache lingered whenever I thought about seeing Nico *the Thug*, as I called him in my head. He was bad news, at least according to Mom and any other grown-up on the planet. Nico and Flavio, together with Peo the Gruff, had been my best friends in elementary school. As much as I wanted to keep it that way, in middle school I would get new classmates.

I asked Viola, "When are you leaving?"

"At the end of the month. College starts in October."

"And Marta?" Viola and her bestie had been inseparable since they were little kids.

"She will be at the Art Academy in Milan."

"Wow! You'll be apart. Aren't you scared to lose touch with her?"

"Never."

I wished I could be as certain about my own friends.

"Dear Jesus, please make my first day of middle school awesome and let me be in the same class with the guys. Make Nico realize how much he missed me, and since you're at it, make him crazy in love with me. I'm not sure what I would do then, but the option for once would be great. Please make my new teachers be nice and like me. And please—"

I stopped when I realized that, out of habit, I was going to ask for a sunny day. Yet, after an enlightening conversation with my uncle Bedo, I had concluded that rain, though unpleasant, was necessary for the survival of the human race.

So I simply added, "Amen" and fell asleep considering how the length of my prayers measured the excitement of days to come.

On the first day of middle grade, I passed my old orange elementary school on my bike like a big shot.

The kids there are so young! Was I one of them only a few months ago?

I crossed the street to the brown middle school building. The glass doors were crowded with prepubescent, rowdy youth, and I felt like a little kid all over again. I locked my bike and joined them.

"Yo, Lee."

I perceived the smile in Nico's words before seeing it on his face. My heart somersaulted in my chest. "Nico! How was summer?"

"Too short." He smirked looking away, puffing at the black hair that hid his big brown eyes. It fell right back. The intense sun of his native Sicily had darkened his olive skin accentuating his gypsy looks.

At eleven, three months could be five years. Yet, every fall when I rejoined my friends, there was no gap as if summer had never happened.

The school doors jerked open and a deluge of kids swept us down the unknown hallways. Janitors in blue scrubs herded the flock. "NO RUNNING! NO YELLING! FIRST YEARS, THIS WAY! COME ALONG!"

Disoriented, I followed the directions without losing sight of Nico's faded t-shirt. We ended up in a big gym where more janitors ordered us to sit on the ground. Flavio grinned and waved at me, his impressive stature making him easy to spot at the back of the sitting bunch. Peo the Gruff sat at his side as always. I pulled Nico's sleeve and pointed at them. He nodded.

A lady with short, blond hair and a mean, green gaze yelled, "QUIET!" She stood in front of the excited crowd. "This is not elementary school anymore!" She didn't make it sound like a good thing. Silence ensued, and she continued, "I am Professor Faramanti."

My blood curdled, recognizing the much-feared name of the woman who had terrorized my sister years before.

Prof. Faramanti carried on, "You will refer to us teachers by our last name, preceded by *Professor*. Also, whenever a *professor* enters the classroom, you will stand up until released to show respect. Is this clear?"

A bewildered silence answered her question.

She repeated, "DID I MAKE MYSELF CLEAR?"

A few voices, not mine, answered, "Yes?"

I was thinking more along the lines of *screw you witch*, glaring at the virago.

She noted, "Goodness gracious! When I ask a question you answer, *yes, ma'am!* Anyway, let's move on. When I call you, stand up and walk to the door. Once your classmates have been called as well, the janitor will take you to your classroom. You will spend there the next three years, provided you don't have to repeat one year or more. Did I make myself clear?"

"Yes, ma'am!" a few more voices answered, again not mine.

Prof. Faramanti was one of the three teachers who had made my big sister's life a nightmare. I could see why. Alarmed, I looked at Nico. He yawned. Through his thug career he had grown accustomed to being yelled at a lot more than I had. He did not seem to care if people liked him, and I envied him for that.

"One A!" Prof. Faramanti called. First year, section A: Viola's old class with her nasty teachers. "Baccellati, Mauro,"

A lanky kid walked to the door. I recognized him from elementary school, but he was shy and I had never spoken to him. He was a lot taller than I remembered. I didn't have time to pray Jesus for my name not to be called.

"Balni, Leda,"

Merda!

I stood up. Nico was unsmiling, wide-eyed. I was doomed to Viola's section with the three witches. I walked to the door by the janitor and turned toward the crowd. Flavio and Peo were staring at me. I nodded their way, like a soldier called to war. They nodded back.

Prof. Faramanti kept calling, and kids stood to reach me: some familiar, like Veronica the Airhead, but what about *my friends*?

"Olani, Laura,"

I had always envied the beautiful blond girl.

Great.

Now she would remind me daily of how ugly and unpopular I was by comparison.

"Partenopeo, Marco,"

Peo's face lit up in a huge grin as he sprung up and reached me by the door, punching my shoulder, and my heart leaped for joy.

"Salisi, Nicolò,"

Nico jumped up raising a fist and screaming, "SCORE!" and performing a victory dance.

Prof. Faramanti yelled, "What part of stand up and walk did you not understand?"

Nico joined us still dancing a little.

A huge grin stretched my face. In a gym full of strangers, three of us were already together. Jesus was on our side. Maybe they were trying to reunite old classmates, which meant Flavio would be next. I stared at him praying under my breath, fists balled up tight.

Prof. Faramanti called, "One B!"

Peo pulled my sleeve. "Lee, we gotta go to class."

"What? But… and Flavio?"

Peo shook his head. Flavio was not in our class. We walked out of the gym. I turned around and saw our tall friend, alone in the crowd, waiting to hear his name, but someone closed the door.

Flavio was our leader, the good guy. I was a nerdy tomboy with a crush on the kid version of the antichrist, Nico the Thug, who was walking beside me, flipping off Bacellati. On my other side Peo, the quiet athlete, smiled.

What was going to happen to us without Flavio?

2

Things Get Weird

When I got home from school Mom, who was not quite the chef, had made sandwiches for lunch.

"So, how did it go?" she asked me, smiling behind one of her many cigarettes.

"Not great, Starry. Flavio's not in my class and I'm in Viola's section."

My sister Viola had called Mom *Starry* after reading *A clockwork Orange* and the nickname had stuck. It meant *old hag*. Starry had gotten over it, since hearing it implied my sister was talking to her, which did not happen often. Viola would have never called her *Mom*, way too corny for my badass sister.

Viola was the first to react to my statement. "My old section? *No way*! Are the three *stronze* still there?"

She had never been jolly, but her gloom had hit record lows since my parents' separation, one year earlier.

Starry prevented my answer. "Watch your mouth, Viola! And Leda, make a good first impression. Viola hated them, but you don't have to."

"I'll keep that in mind," I answered, biting into my sandwich with *prosciutto* and *mozzarella*.

Viola crooked an eyebrow over her big, hazel eyes. "*Really*, Starry? You think it was *me*?"

She had grown into a copy of Mom, skinny and with gorgeous olive skin covered by a generous layer of makeup. However, she inherited Dad's perfect sight. Also, she permed her straight brown hair into wavy curls, the only (fake) resemblance between us.

"I didn't say it was you," Starry answered, level. Fuzzer, our fat cat, circumnavigated the kitchen table like a shark but a lot louder.

Viola didn't relent. "Do you remember when that art *stronza* Solani assigned us *to represent a metaphor with mixed media?* At *twelve*?"

Starry smirked behind her glasses. "I don't, but she *is* a tad crazy."

Viola scoffed. "A *tad*? I had to ask Dad for help!"

The detail was revealing because Viola excelled in art. She had desired nothing more than to attend art high school with her best friend Marta, but Dad had forbidden it, deeming it unsuitable for finding a job.

Dad himself was an engineer by day but a gifted artist whenever not at work. So, Viola had trudged through a private high school specialized in foreign languages and was now ready to move on to college.

Fuzzer meowed, and I snuck him a small piece of *prosciutto* under the table.

Viola continued, "Dad made this amazing metaphoric drawing of dawn with ink, watercolors and pencils. It showed a wooden mannequin driving a chariot through the sky, bringing day over a dark countryside landscape."

"Wow, that doesn't sound like a twelve-year-old's piece of work," I commented.

Viola answered, "It didn't look like one either! But Prof. Solani's expectations exceeded a twelve-year-old's skills by far."

"Did you get an A?" I asked. Starry puffed at her cigarette, her sandwich uneaten.

"Nope. The *stronza* scribbled in bright red: *D, a mannequin riding a chariot is not a metaphor of dawn.* Can you believe her?" I couldn't, and Viola added, "Worse! She wrote her sour comment *on* the drawing, ruining Dad's work!"

I swallowed, "And Prof. Visoni?"

"She hated me, period."

Starry sighed. "On a different topic, Viola, did you speak to my friend Vanna?"

"Yes—"

I interrupted her, "Why would you? Did you meet her?"

My sister explained, "Not yet, but she lives in Padua and might have a place for me to live in when I move there for college."

"She does?" Starry and I asked at the same time.

"Yes!" Viola answered, "She owns several properties."

"True," Starry confirmed. "She's always been well-off."

"*Anyway*," Viola resumed. "Among her many, expensive properties, she owns a house that is falling apart. She rented it to an old lady for decades. When the granny died, Vanna realized the place was a mess. She can't rent it unless she throws a lot of money into it, but she can let me and two other students squat for a modest fee."

"But, is it *safe*?" Starry asked, wrinkles marrying her tall forehead.

"Oh, yeah! It's just little things… The paint is peeling, cosmetic stuff. Nothing dangerous," Viola belittled.

"Mm," Starry said. "You'd better show me this place soon."

"Can't wait to see it myself! I should be able to move in two weeks!"

Mom cringed. "Already? I'll go with you, then. I have to take the Group Dynamic's final, anyway."

Mom had gone back to college herself one year earlier, and was doing stellar so far, trying to escape her disastrous housewife career. Dad hated the idea and despised Starry's major: Psychology. She argued this had been one of many reasons for their separation, but according to Dad the blame lay on the therapist who had filled Mom's head with *crazy ideas and unrealistic expectations*. No wonder Dad had thrown a fit when Viola had announced she would become yet another shrink.

Viola rolled her eyes. "Starry, let's make this clear. I'd rather *not* see you in Padua… I'm not a big fan of the *going to college with Mom* idea, you know? We're getting the same degree, but let's keep it between us. Thank god you don't attend classes."

Starry sighed, and I cleared plates from the table.

"Dear Jesus, please spare me from the wrath of the three mean witches that made Viola's life a nightmare and let me sleep well with no nightmares. Amen."

When recess started on our second day, everyone

poured into the hallway, but I stayed back drawing at my desk. Outside the classroom boys were chasing girls, a primal behavior triggered by Italian TV, which objectified gorgeous women and ridiculed the rest.

For example, in *Striscia La Notizia* models in skimpy clothes brought the news to male presenters and clueless floozies who wanted nothing but sex with ugly men crowded Italian comedies like *Rimini-Rimini.*

Bodacious ladies swarmed even my favorite cartoons like *Lupin the Third,* where the main hero seduced and abandoned them with no second thought. Not to mention *Colpo Grosso,* a late night strip-tease show that every kid snuck out of bed to watch at least once in a lifetime. So much for the Catholic country where no one spoke about sex.

So the boys ran after the pretty girls, who screeched away following the script learned from our sensuality-doped TV. If a male caught up with his prey, he slapped her butt and fled.

Before this odd behavior, I had always been at home with the guys, but now I belonged nowhere. I would not cheer them feeling other ladies' butts, and no one would chase me, Lee the tomboy, more so after I beat up Nico for trying in fifth grade. I had wrecked my career as a girl then, which caused me as much pride as regret.

Peo's voice startled me. "What's up?"

He leaned on my desk, back toward me, arms crossed. I could only see his short, black hair and broad shoulders.

A smile spread across my face. "Not much, Peo, you?"

"Eh."

"It's not like old times anymore, huh?"

"Of course it is!" Nico answered from behind me, startling me. He was skilled at sneaking on people.

Peo and Nico didn't like each other. Both Peo and I were close to Flavio and Nico joined our group when moved next to me in fourth grade. Without Flavio, our leader and our glue, things were getting weirder, at least for me. Peo and Nico seemed to be making new friends. Me… not so much.

Peo said, scowling at Nico, "Well, take care." He took off from my desk and stepped out of the classroom as I stared at his back. Was this goodbye?

Nico sighed, slouching on the chair next to mine, hands crossed behind the nape of his neck. "Man, he's smitten."

"*He's what*?" I asked.

"Smitten. Peo, I mean, isn't it obvious?"

I burst out laughing because Peo the Gruff did not strike me as the romantic type. "And who'd be the lucky one?"

Nico turned to look me in the eye, raising an eyebrow. "Aren't you supposed to be the smart one, Lee?"

I used to be, but in this world of boys and girls everyone had caught up with me and was way ahead. I had nothing left. Nico stood up, patted me on a shoulder and walked out of the classroom, too.

After recess I shuddered, waiting for notorious art professor Solani. I heard the dreaded sound of heels approaching from the hallway, and the chattering in the classroom died. We stared at the door, except for Nico who kept throwing paper balls at Baccellati's head. I was imagining the forty-something blonde with short hair and heavy make up, and I remained stunned when a mousy woman entered instead.

We all stood up as instructed. *This* would be our art teacher. I could not believe my luck. The evil art witch was around and she still taught in my section; so what? Maybe Jesus was trying to make it up to me after forgetting Flavio out of our class. Not even close, but I appreciated the gesture.

The hour went by fast, leaving me to face my last menace: Prof. Visoni. We all stood up like little soldiers as she sashayed her way into the classroom. Bright blue eyeshadow contrasted with her mop of black tight curls, surrounding her long face and beak nose. She burst into loud, unnecessary laughter, waving her hand as if we were a cheering crowd.

She said, "Sit down already. Ha, ha! You're such cuties. Let's see who we have here." A cloy cloud of perfume followed her entrance.

She started roll call, "Mauro Baccellati,"

"Here!"

"Leda Balni,"

I was going to reply when she added, "*Balni*? Like *Viola Balni*?" The abundant foundation on her cheeks almost cracked. "Was Viola your sister?"

"She still *is*," I answered.

"Ha, ha, ha! Of course, *silly*!" Her hideous glare conveyed no playfulness.

I hated her on the spot, perhaps from even before I met her, through my sister's agony, but I regretted my smart-mouth remark. I wasn't doing half a decent job of making a good impression.

Prof. Visoni didn't seem to mind. "Oh, she was such a cute, intelligent girl!" she added in a sickening display of flattery and flirtation. She batted her eyelashes heavy with mascara, swaying back and forth in front of the class.

Cazzarola. Given the way she treated my sister, what the heck does she do to the kids she does not like?

Worse, the jealous glares of my new classmates pinned me to my desk.

Visoni blurted, "But you're even *cuter*! Leda. I'll *remember that.*" She stared at me and the hair on the back of my neck bristled.

She moved on with roll call, making students uncomfortable at every chance she had. I wished for one of her heels to break and send her flying headlong in front of the kids she was entertaining herself with. When she left, her chemical fumes lingered like a radioactive cloud, invisible yet noxious, perpetrating the anxiety hanging over the whole class. We had survived Chernobyl, hopefully this would pass, too.

3

A Very Old Grudge

A few weeks passed. The wind snatched more rotten leaves from the trees shivering in the constant rain that plagued the Po Valley from September till March. No wonder it used to be a swamp.

October begun and Prof. Faramanti, who taught us math and science, after the digestive and respiratory systems had to explain reproduction.

I gave her my full attention. She spent a great deal of time talking about *hormones*, how they were the culprit of all unpleasant changes that people underwent either through puberty or on a monthly basis.

Hormones made teenagers angry, sad, and hairy. We were all impressed. When Faramanti ran out of preambles and stared at the anatomy figures on our textbook, she seemed hesitant, not so sure herself.

"So, the male reproductive system… This is, um, the penis." Everyone giggled.

Nico said, "Mine's bigger."

Romeo, the kid sitting beside him, yelled, "*Boom*!"

Faramanti ignored them both.

Nico and Romeo had founded a little delinquent association, getting away with anything thanks to their angelic, pretty faces. Nico had learned from Romeo to be more subtle while Romeo had learned from Nico that there were no limits to what he could accomplish behind a charming smile. Their attitude reminded me of the Siamese cats from *Lady and the Tramp*. Both Nico and Romeo had big brown eyes. Yet, while Romeo had a round face with short, brown hair that made him look like an angel, Nico's longer black hair and dimpled chin made him look like everything but.

Prof. Faramanti muttered under her breath. Her embarrassment was appropriate given that the topic was something you should *never* talk about. That was at least what I had gathered from years of church and hearing *you'll understand when you grow up*.

I hadn't understood, yet.

Faramanti proceeded, "This is not too different

from, um, plant pollination, which we've already talked about. The one thing I want to mention is *menstruation*…"

She illustrated how young girls bleed once a month, from their hoo-has.

"But why?" I asked, appalled. "Why don't boys bleed too?"

Blondie, as I called my irritating neighbor to her dismay, chimed in, "Grandma told me it's because of Eve and the original sin!"

Wow, bleeding five days a month for a stolen apple seems rough.

"Ah," Faramanti replied, "No, it's just the way it is. Women make eggs—"

"Like chickens!" Romeo yelled from the back, and the boys snickered.

Nico's neighbor was as cute as he was short and arrogant, and I could not stand him.

Faramanti didn't laugh. "Well, yes. That's what chicken eggs are for. If the rooster fecundates the hen, chicks will be born."

"*Gross*! And we *eat* them?" Maria, a skinny, pretty girl with deep blue eyes asked, looking paler than usual.

Faramanti huffed. "You eat chickens too, don't you? Women make eggs, and un*used* ones have to be, ah, disposed of through bleeding."

"Eeeew!" Disgust rose from the males in the class while the girls seemed too horrified to utter any sound.

Prof. Faramanti rolled her eyes, her mouth twisted in a grimace. “There is nothing gross about it! That's how the species survives!”

I heard Nico whispering to Romeo, “I bet you she’s bleeding right now.”

Coglione.

Romeo made a disgusted face, and I wished I were a male.

Prof. Faramanti continued, “Now we have cleared that out. Here’s what we will do. Take your notebook and copy all the figures from this chapter, names and all. Color them in, too.”

So, I enthusiastically drew a scientific-looking collection of willies and hoo-has, except that now they were penises and vaginas, from every possible point of view, inside and outside.

At recess everyone chatted about the peculiar lecture that had created more questions than answers. No one dared to ask them to the teacher, so they bounced amongst us with the most bewildering results.

Baccellati, the lanky kid who had become the unlucky target of Nico, Romeo, and the other bullies in the class, walked towards me. “Did you understand what Faramanti was talking about?” he asked.

"What part?" *Penises? Vaginas?*

"The whole bleeding thing," he elaborated, blushing and brushing some invisible spec off his shirt.

"Ah, somewhat. *Why*?"

His gaze shifted from his feet to the window and back. "So, I wasn't paying a lot of attention..." His interest kind of moved me. Most boys had just cringed. "So, will I bleed, too?" he asked.

"Ah, no. Only women do."

"Are you *sure*? Because she called them MENstruation..."

"Yeah, I asked." I fought to keep a straight face.

"Awesome!" he screamed, dancing away without thanking me. *Stronzo*. I should have laughed at him when I had the chance.

Later that afternoon, I was in front of the TV at home, when the doorbell rang. I ran to answer and had to do a double take when I faced a stranger, *female*, more or less my age, standing behind the gate of our front yard.

I knew no girls. All my friends were boys. "Ye*s*?" I asked.

She said, "Ah, hi. Can I... come in? I would like to ask you *something*."

A prank, Nico's, for sure. I pushed the button that opened the gate and met the newcomer mid-way into the front yard. We shook hands, studying each other.

"Sonia," said the tall girl, big green eyes glowing in a round face framed by strawberry blond curls.

"Hi, I'm Leda, but everyone calls me Lee. So?"

Hands in my pockets, I glared at her. I had been lonely, but didn't want to pass for a fool when she revealed the hoax. Also, I wanted to go back inside to watch *Voltron, Defender Of The Universe* as soon as possible.

Sonia hesitated. "Well, my ball fell past your hedge. Can I get it? And… can you show me your yard while we're at it? It looks like the biggest in the Pro."

The Pro, short for Prototype, was our little gated community of a hundred houses. It was the first of many identical ones that made the bulk of the more recent part of Arese, our town just outside Milan in the northern Italian countryside.

I nodded. "Sure, there isn't much to see." I wondered how she had gotten the ball into my garden, playing by herself.

As we climbed up the slope in the front yard to turn around the house and fetch the ball, Sonia chatted me up. She was twelve, one year older than me, and attended my same school, except that she was in section C.

My heart stopped. "Ah, do you know Flavio, in 1C?"

She thought about it. "No, I don't know too many first-year students. Is he your *boyfriend*?"

"Hell, *no*! Just a friend." I blushed.

What a bad topic.

We passed the silver maple, the swing, and the hammock and turned on the back, outside the kitchen.

"Is he cute?" Sonia inquired.

"Yeah, he's cute." I admitted, feeling weird about it. Sonia was sturdy and amused, a mischievous smile brightening her face.

"I'll keep an eye out for him, then!" She winked.

Let her have him. I don't care, do I?

"That's it," I said waving at the yard, expecting a trick anytime now.

Sonia asked, "What do you do when you get home from school? I play tennis."

"Um, I watch cartoons, read, and climb trees."

"I read, too! Do you like Mickey Mouse?"

"No, I hate his guts. I prefer Fethry Duck."

Sonia laughed, "Mickey Mouse is the hero! Fethry Duck is dumb."

"Fethry Duck is *nice*. Mickey Mouse is pedantic, boring, and annoying."

Kinda like Romeo.

I hated perfect heroes. I was more of an underdog type of person, perhaps because heroes never noticed me.

"Pedantic? Is that another character?" Sonia asked.

"No, pedantic means...." I hesitated, feeling as obnoxious as freaking Mickey Mouse. "A know-it-all."

"Why, you sure say some big words."

I gloated, even if Sonia looked more bored than impressed. No need to tell her about my abominable ignorance of history and geography, my rage fits during which I transformed into my eviler self Mr Hyde, that monsters terrified me, and that, much to Dad's disappointment, I had never played tennis in my life because it would bend further my crooked back.

"Well, can we play tennis together sometime?" Sonia asked, fetching her ball and somehow looking up at me through her lashes in spite of being much taller than me.

"Ah, yeah. Right, sure," I lied.

Sonia lowered her eyes. "So, can I buzz you again?"

"Ah, yeah. Right, sure," I repeated.

She left.

No hoax. Ha. Voltron had been long done. Dazed, I stared through the glass front door at the back of the girl who would turn my nerdy, lonely life upside down.

"Dear Jesus, I am sorry about the original sin, but isn't holding a grudge for two thousand years a sin as well? I mean, I don't want to sound critical with you being perfect and all. You did one amazing job at creating *everything*. Fixing the bleeding problem would seem minor, but what do I know? Well, if I end up bleeding, please give me at least big boobs to go with it. And please let me sleep well with no nightmares. Amen."

4

Fictional Geography

A week later, Prof. Faramanti brought back our corrected tests on the reproductive system. Some red marks on my rendition of the male apparatus surprised me.

"What's wrong with this?" I asked, puzzled.

"Ah, Balni, yes. See, the scrotum and the penis are, um, separated, you drew them all together as one big lump, but the scrotum hangs loose."

"It does?"

"Yes."

"And it doesn't fall off?"

She blushed. "Balni, nevermind. You'll understand when you grow up."

Really?

The mystery remained unsolved.

The next period we had Geography. I was awful at pretending I did not hate Visoni's guts, but the more I showed her contempt, the more she tried to win me over. She only made me sick to my stomach every time I smelled her cloy perfume.

At least I was not the only one on her pet list: Romeo, Nico's neighbor, kept me good company. Visoni had just called Romeo out with Blondie to quiz them.

"And what's the tallest mountain in Italy, Martelli?"

Blondie answered, "Mont Blanc, 4,810 meters."

"Romeo, what's the wealthiest region in Italy?"

Romeo pondered, "Ah, well, the one with more money."

Visoni, who would have snatched off Blondie's head for such an answer, nodded encouraging. "Therefore…"

"The one with more business?" Visoni giggled and nodded. Romeo, shameless, asked, "Ah, are we talking about legal business only or illegal as well?"

Visoni laughed out loud. "Ha, ha, ha! You are sooo cute. No, honey, legal only."

"Well, then I guess, Lombardy?"

"So close! More north."

This was ridiculous.

"Ah, well. Trentino?"

"Excellent!"

Blondie got a C, Romeo an A.

Romeo approached me at recess, which was unheard of. "A teacher's pet's life rocks, Balni, doesn't it?"

I retorted, "Are you serious? I can't believe you go along with it! How can you stand her?"

A glint of mischief lit up his brown eyes, all lashes. "Are you kidding me? It's a free for all!" He was only a couple of inches taller than me, and I was the shortest in the universe, but he didn't seem to mind.

"No, Romeo, only for you and me. Everyone else has to study, and they never get more than a C."

"But we're all that matters, aren't *we*?" He batted his long lashes at me. By *we* he clearly did not mean the two of us but his royal self.

I insisted, "Doesn't it seem wrong to you that while we get away with anything, she dooms everyone else to mediocrity, at least grade-wise, no matter what they do?"

"Me-dio-crity," he imitated me in a stupid voice. "Not one bit, and boy, Balni, are you nerdy. I would have never said so with your tough-girl attitude."

Nico startled me. "Don't let that fool ya, bro, and yeah, Lee's always been bad at juicing life." Nico approached. I could not believe he was siding with

Romeo, rather than with me.

"What are you talking about?" I retorted, knowing he meant that I sucked at having fun. It hurt because it rang true. He knew me so well and yet did not like me while I still liked him quite a bit and detested myself even more for it.

Meanwhile Nico echoed in the same dumb voice Romeo had used earlier, "*What are you talking about?*"

Furious, I blurted, "You two deserve each other. I'm out!"

"... of your mind!" Romeo tacked on in a singsong voice. They guffawed and exchanged a high five walking toward the hallway leaving me alone with my melancholy.

As hanging out with my *male* friends was not an option anymore, I saw Sonia more and more. When the weather allowed, we played volleyball over the big gate in her driveway, but the approaching winter had made it almost impossible. I loved volleyball. Drawn to it by Japanese cartoons, I had played with Dad at the park during the weekends we spent together.

Sonia proposed, "Why don't we play for real, like *Mila and Shiro*?"

The cartoon she was talking about was one of my favorites. "That would be awesome! But where?" There were no sports in Italian schools, just tedious studying.

"Well, I saw an advertisement outside the gym; the oratory is recruiting girls our age. If you ask your parents, I will ask mine."

"Sounds awesome, but… isn't the net, like, super tall?"

Sonia snickered. "Well, I can be Mila, and *you* can be her short sidekick."

"Right," I answered.

I didn't want to be a sidekick nor I wanted to be short. I wanted to be the main character of my own cartoon and, for once, I wanted to get the guy, too.

The following Thursday morning, Blondie asked, "Ready for the geography test?"

"The *what*?" I answered in shock.

"The geography test, Balni. Geez, did you forget?"

I fumbled through the pages of my planner to the current date where the sentence of my doom stared back at me in my own writing. I hadn't checked. As usual, I hadn't done my homework, spending the afternoons playing video games, training with my new volleyball team, and then watching cartoons with Sonia.

I pulled out the geography book. "What's the test on?" I asked, frantic, leafing through chapters.

Blondie rolled her eyes. "Lombardy, Trentino, and Veneto. Good luck," she said without sympathy.

Just then, Visoni entered the classroom in a cloud of her nuclear spring perfume.

We all stood up.

"Sit down, cuties! Desks apart and books away. It's fun time!"

Panic engulfed me.

What am I gonna do? Pretend to be sick?

She wrote three questions on the board, one on Lombardy's economy, one on Trentino's geography, and the third on Veneto's population.

Everyone scribbled on their tests while I stared at my blank paper in shock. Visoni looked at me with a huge smile, and I pretended to get to work, feeling very healthy and guilty like hell. She turned away, and I reached for the book under my desk. I slid it on my lap and fumbled through the pages as quietly as I could. I didn't even know where to look. Blondie glared in my direction. I closed the text and put it back in its place. Despair overtook me.

Wake up, wake up, WAKE UP! What am I gonna do?

Tears welled up in my eyes. I did not wake. Visoni would find out I was an idiot, and somehow, even her detested opinion mattered.

I looked around the class for help, finding none. My gaze paused on Nico: legs extended under his desk, hands crossed behind his head, a big yawn stretching his gypsy features into an obvious grimace of boredom. He turned toward me as if he sensed my gaze on him and grinned giving me the thumbs up.

Visoni yelled, "Nico! Stop bothering your classmates and write something for once, will you?" She turned toward me to smile.

I will never forget the juxtaposition of her fake smile and Nico's middle finger, right behind her back. He flipped her off then broke into another yawn, resuming his lounging.

When Visoni turned away, I had a new resolve. Nico had survived years of school without ever studying; I would not die on my first slip up. True, every year it looked like he would fail and repeat, but he never had, yet.

I looked at my blank paper. If I was going out, I would do so with a bang. So I invented the economy of Lombardy. For heaven's sake, I lived in it: stupid fashion, cars, industries littering the countryside. I remembered my field trip to Lake Maggiore and threw tourism into the mix. All my statements, although written in my best style and vocabulary, were very vague. So I added random numbers close to each category I discussed, for example deciding that fashion was 33% of the revenue. I moved on to Trentino. I spent most of my summers there at Grandma's house in Afes, so I illustrated its mountainous geography, the apple orchards, a few vineyards. To give Trentino credibility, I invented the heights of some mountains. Mont Blanc came to mind from one of the latest oral examinations and I added its height at 6,850 meters. That seemed tall enough. At the end of the test I handed my work to Prof. Visoni without looking her in the eye. I had survived so far; there was time to worry about consequences.

Several days later, Visoni sashayed her way into the classroom. A shiver ran down my spine when I saw the stack of graded assignments in her arms. Brutal red scars marred the white and blue paper sky of our ignorance. I searched her face for disappointment and anger, but I only found her usual fake smile and a lot of make up.

"Sit down, please! Here are your tests, *lovelies*, as pitiful as ever. Did you open the book at least? You waste my time by having me read your garbage, but alas! I have to grade you. So here you go, this is what you're worth."

Oh, I hate her, I hate her so much!

At least I hoped that after bombing the test she would remove me from her pet list. When she called my name, I stood up like a robot, heart trying to leave my chest, an uncomfortable warm tide bathing my fear and guilt. I stepped toward her, stealing glances at her face, but she beamed, handing back my work of fictional geography. I snatched it and turned around to regain the safety of my chair, where I cringed and looked: "A".

Did I guess geography? Am I psychic?

A huge smile stretched on my face. Blondie glanced sideways, trying to get a glimpse of my grade. I turned to her. "Blondie, what's the height of Mont Blanc?"

She huffed. "You know my name is Sasha, right?" I didn't answer, and she continued, "I don't remember, we did Val D'Aosta a while back, but it's the tallest in Italy, above 4,000 meters."

My blood stopped circulating.

"Ah. Thank you," I answered.

Forget the height of the freaking mountain, which I had missed by an abundant 2,000 meters; it wasn't even in Trentino! I looked again at my paper: not one red mark, except the A glinting on the first page.

Then I realized; Prof. Visoni hadn't even *read* my paper. A boiling rage made its way to Mr. Hyde, awakening my uglier self from its torpor. I was at a crossroad; was I going to keep my undeserved A, or was I going to unmask the lazy *stronza* for what she was?

Justice shall be done.

As in a trance, I stood up, my fictional geography test tight in my hand. I stomped to Visoni's desk, indignation erupting from my every pore. In spite of common sense and my screaming survival instinct, I yelled at her, "This is ridiculous! *A*? Did you even read my paper? Mont Blanc, height and all?"

Screw being the teacher's pet!

The collective "Gasp!" confirmed my rioter status. Visoni's heavily made up facade fractured, her hideous smile faltering. Time stood still, no one breathed. I would get suspended, and I hoped she would lose her job. I would avenge Viola.

She cocked an eyebrow in surprise, then recovered. "Oh my, Lee, so angry!" She took my paper and scribbled on it, then she handed it to me. "Here you go, sweetie, calm down, okay? Cremoni!" she called the next kid to pick up his work.

In a trance I moved back to my desk, sat down and looked at my test: "A+."

I would not be suspended. She would keep her job. I had lost a bit of my dignity. Was there even such a grade as an A+?

"Dear Jesus, I am so sorry that I forgot to study

and tried to cheat. Thanks for having my back again, but please, I'd rather no one thought of me as a teacher's pet. Please make me a volleyball champion, like Mila—" I paused, proud of my newly formulated prayer. "And please make me happy tomorrow. Amen."

5

Locker Break

On Wednesday, I walked into the girls' locker room with the crowd to get ready for our two hours of phys ed.

Blondie trotted toward her friends: Maria, ineffable ballerina of unmatched smarts, and her sidekick Claudia, a freckly red-head with bright hazel eyes. I smirked as Blondie tried to fit into her friends' conversation, but they barely noticed. She reminded me of my pitiful attempts to impress Viola.

"OH MY GOD! Romeo's *so hot*!" Claudia declared removing her pants, her long smooth hair bouncing up and down. Uproar from everyone else confirmed that Romeo was the real thing.

"Hotter than Nico?" Laura the Gorgeous

prompted, taking off her t-shirt and raising an eyebrow. She was the most popular girl among first-years, and I envied her with all my might. Everyone nodded in agreement that this was a tough problem.

"I like Mario in 1B," Veronica the Airhead confessed, glossy-eyed, hugging her sweats.

"Like that's news!" chimed in one of her friends. Everyone laughed, patting Veronica on the back. Her face reddened, but she joined in the laughter. Then she gathered her courage and asked, "And you, Maria? Are you in the Romeo club?"

Everyone turned toward Maria, who blushed and lowered her blue eyes in that very adorable way I was ashamed to learn and therefore despised.

"Ah, well," she hesitated.

"Oh, come on!" Claudia nudged her.

Blondie sighed, "I'm in the Romeo club, for sure."

Nobody acknowledged her answer, eyes still glued on Maria, who said, "No, not the Romeo club." She stared at the floor, then she mumbled, "I kind of like Nico."

"And who doesn't?" claimed a short girl, friends with Veronica. "He's the bad boy!"

While the other girls whispered and giggled, an unexpected jolt of pain had my heart in a spasm.

Nico the Thug, my old friend. Nico with the

gypsy eyes, Nico the saxophone player. I wondered if they even imagined. We had become friends when nobody thought he could have any, when nobody liked him. Now he had a fan club.

The bad boy who had fondled my butt. Was I jealous? The red bracelet on my wrist itched. I was ashamed of wishing for Flavio to declare his love for me. We hadn't talked in weeks and I didn't miss him as much. I missed more our old gang and the sense of belonging somewhere. Flavio and I had been friends. I stared at the bracelet a second longer before ripping it off.

"Hello, Ladies!" Nico screamed, jumping out of the shower stall where he had been hiding.

The locker room exploded in a welter of screeching, confusion, and half-naked girls.

He hurtled to the exit, slapping a few butts on his path to salvation, which turned out to be a mirage because right outside the locker room he collided with gigantic De Prori, professor of phys ed.

Nico absorbed the impact falling backward on his *culo*, toward our open door, which slammed close between hysterical screams.

In the unnatural silence that followed, the voice of Prof. De Prori rumbled Nico's last name, echoing through the still empty gym, "SALISI!"

I ran to open the door a sliver to peek. The other girls emitted ultrasonic whispers, "Noooooooo! Balni, what are you doing?"

I didn't acknowledge them and after a few seconds they crowded the opening to get a glimpse themselves.

De Prori had his back toward us and could not see the totem pole of heads piling up behind the door, ajar. He was dragging Nico out of the gym, probably to the principal's office.

I closed the door. At least my brooding on my sad, non-existent love life had resulted in me not having taken off my clothes. Viola would have despised my attempt to find a bright side.

Maria was still standing in her underwear and a t-shirt, a hand clasped over her mouth, face on fire, eyes wide open.

She blurted, at no one in particular, "Oh my God, do you think he heard what I said?"

"No," I answered to calm her down. "I barely did, and I was right there."

He could have heard her, but what was the point? Like Grandma said, no point in crying over the spilled milk.

"Anyway," Claudia interjected studying me. "How come you ripped off your red bracelet, Balni?" Her freckled face was alight with mischief. "Red is for love. So who does tough Balni like?"

All eyes turned to me. The silence I was hoping would turn into boredom heightened the suspense. I could sense Blondie's hatred. She would have done anything for the spotlight, and I would have done anything to pass it on to her. I remained stuck in the middle of the locker room, with my broken heart in my hand in the form of a red cotton thread. I could not admit to liking Nico, when it was obvious he would never like me back, so I opted for lying, the thing I was worst at. "Ah, no. It broke. It was old."

"Yeah, right. Well then, what was your wish? Because if it broke it will come true!"

I was about to say I couldn't tell when a violent knocking almost shook the door off its hinges.

Prof. De Prori yelled, "OUT OF THE DARN LOCKER ROOM, RIGHT NOW! OR I SWEAR TO GOD I'LL HAVE YOU RUN THE WHOLE TWO HOURS!"

I slipped into my shorts, and we all rushed out into the gym.

Prof. De Prori looked like a furious version of Lurch, from *The Addams Family*. "SILENCE! DISPOSE YOURSELF IN A LINE IN ALPHABETICAL ORDER!"

Confused and alarmed, we tried to line up without making too much noise. Nico was still M.I.A.

"What happened today is *unacceptable*!" Prof. De Prori thundered. "I will tolerate no such behavior, *ever*! From now on you have two minutes to change in the locker rooms. TWO MINUTES!" He reiterated, screaming. "Every extra minute you take, even just one of you, will turn into five extra minutes of running for the whole class! *Understood*?"

We all stared, terrified.

"UNDERSTOOD?" He screamed, and I thought he would pop a coronary.

"Yes," some of us answered.

"YES, SIR! For Pete's sake! *Understood*?" he asked a last time.

"YES, SIR!" we all answered, glad to make him less unhappy.

"Now, run! It will be a long day."

Laura protested, "Wait a minute, we were *victims*! Why are *we* running?"

Prof. De Prori transformed into an uglier, angrier self, which seemed impossible. "Ten more minutes of running for the stupid question! Anyone else?"

We ran. Someone grumbled about injustice.

"FIVE MINUTES MORE!" he yelled. "I swear, if anyone talks, I'll have you all leave this gym crawling!"

No one else spoke.

October 11 was the infamous day of *San Firmino*, Saint Fermin (a feast for every freshman). Tradition had it that, on the doomed day, older students armed themselves with permanent markers and covered freshmen or anyone who'd let them with indecent writings, insults, mustaches, and worse.

Teachers overlooked the barbaric tradition, which was allegedly consequent to the resemblance of *Fermin* to *firma*: *signature* in Italian.

For the first few years of elementary school I had taken refuge at Viola's side, who attended middle school back then. When my sister had moved on to her private high school in Milan, I was older and stuck with my buddies, avoiding the worst.

This year I didn't stand a chance; I was on my own and I was a freshman. I wore my oldest clothes and went to school ready to face battle. To my surprise, I made my way to our class unscathed, wading among herds of markers, choirs of derision, and cries of defeat. My steps became slower and heavier. Had I become invisible?

Two strangers approached me, marker drawn and the classic grin of the wrongdoer, but my famous glare, which I thought had lost much of its power, was enough to send them veering toward easier prey.

I dropped my book bag by my desk, when a familiar voice chanted, almost whispered in my ear, "Baaalniii! You know what's cooomiiing!"

"Nico, one move and I'll bite your face off."

I turned around, my icy gaze melting in his amusement. I freaking blushed and pretended to get something out of my bag. In spite of the historical precedent during which, in fifth grade, I had bit off Nico's arm, the kid seemed fearless. I loved that.

His skit at the gym had almost cost him suspension, but he had gotten away with a warning. Likely the teachers dreaded keeping him around an extra year as much as he did.

He smiled. "Come on, pen only. You can wash it off later."

"Well, if I get signed, so do you, buddy."

"Deal! Give me your arm."

"No way. I know you're a cheater, Nico! At the same time."

"*Me*? A cheater? I wasn't the one leafing through the geography book during the test, you know? I earn my Fs," Nico said.

Ouch. That hurt.

Rather than getting defensive I gave him an explanation. "Listen, it's not my fault if the crazy V took me and your new best bud under her wing," I explained as I signed my name on his arm.

"I know, I know," he answered, without contesting that Romeo was his new best friend, which hurt a little, too. "I see no one signed you yet," he noticed while writing on my arm.

I shrugged. "Same for you."

The bell rang and Romeo's voice surprised both of us. "How sweet! Don't tell me you guys have something going. Wouldn't that be perfect?"

Can't I ever be happy for one minute?

"Shut up, Romeo!" I hissed.

Nico said nothing, finishing to sign my arm.

Romeo raised his hands. "Just saying what I see, that's all." He dropped into his seat as everyone trickled in for classes.

Insults, mustaches, and less appropriate body parts covered Baccellati, Nico's favorite victim, who sat at his desk simmering in thoughts of revenge easy to guess even behind the filth that covered his face.

How could I like Nico when he could be such a *stronzo*?

The first three hours of class trudged by in the restless excitement characteristic of Saint Fermin. At recess everyone poured into the hallways, but I stuck to doodling on my planner. Rather than the fits of rage that had characterized my childhood, I was more prone to a steady, growing discomfort. I still liked to isolate myself. With no trees to hide in, I disappeared into my drawings, anesthetizing my brain and avoiding confrontation with my peers. I didn't know what I was, what they thought I was, or what I should be. So, I doodled away.

When Nico leaned on my desk, my breath hitched. Everyone was out in the hallway partaking in the big Saint Fermin fight.

What the heck does he want?

Nico asked, "So? Are you gonna stay holed up in here all recess? You're not afraid, are you?"

"Of course not, but I—" How could I explain my awkward position to Nico the Thug? Buddies didn't whine, so I opted to change the topic. "Man, did you see how mellow our art teacher is? I was so surprised we didn't get Prof. Solani!" I did not add more epithets to the big *stronza* who had scribbled a red D on the front of Viola's and Dad's artwork because of Nico's incredulous stare.

"You were *surprised*?" he spluttered out.

"You weren't?"

"Lee, Prof. Solani is *my mother*, that's why she's not our art teacher. She can't grade her own spawn."

"*What*?"

He chuckled. Holy freaking cow! Nico was the son of mad art teacher Prof. Solani and the gray hairy monster I had met only once in my life, thank God and all the Saints. Nico the Thug made a lot more sense and I found myself indebted a little less to Jesus and a little more to Nico.

"Wow," I added, still in shock. "And she kept her last name?"

"Yeah, well, please don't advertise it around too much. I'd rather not add my mom to the reasons people want to beat me."

"Sure thing, man. I've got your back."

"Cool. So, not like I don't enjoy chatting about my birthrights, but a lot of sad girls are waiting for me in the hallway. Are you coming out or what?"

"What for? Without Flavio… things changed."

"Flavio?" Nico frowned then said, "Oh, come on! We're like *Lupin the Third* and his gang. We're not always together, but we're always friends!"

The comparison made me smile. "Oh yeah? And who would you be?"

"Lupin, of course!"

I laughed, because Nico behaved like Lupin, the thief with a soft spot for the ladies. Nico continued the similitude counting on his fingers. "Flavio is the wise samurai Goemon, Peo is taciturn Jigen, and of course you're Fujiko!"

"Me? Yeah, right!" I rebuked, laughing since the bodacious, flirty girlfriend of Lupin was nothing like me.

Wait a second…

Nico added, "Okay, a flat-chested version of Fujiko,"

"You *moron*! I'm not that easy!"

He rolled his eyes, huffing. "Oh yeah, I forgot. You're a *nun*."

Nun was the derogatory monicker boys reserved for girls who did not frolic with boys. The assumption was that if a girl turned down a boy the whole male gender must repulse her —except

Jesus of course.

I had never turned down Nico or anyone. No one had ever asked. Nico walked away leaving me abash with my two options in this new world of girls and boys: I was either easy or a nun. Neither felt like me. I swallowed back the tears and disappeared once again in my doodles.

6

Bad Things Come in Three

After recess we had math. Faramanti was blabbering away about some theorem, and I was doodling on my planner when I got mail. The note folded on my desk read on its top, "4 Maria."

I took the piece of paper and balanced on the back legs of my chair to hand the note to its rightful owner, sitting behind me, and resumed my neat handiwork. A minute later Maria tapped on my shoulder. Gaze on the teacher, I pretended to scratch the back of my head clutching the message instead. The address read, "4 Lee."

Ha.

When I read the note a sharp, cold pain pierced through me. It said, "YIKES!!! Nico ASKED ME!!! WHAT DO I DO?!?"

The emotion of the plethora of capitalization, exclamations, and question marks, contrasted with Maria's neat calligraphy. *Nico asked me* meant he wanted them to *be* boyfriend and girlfriend.

The echo of my crashing heart still resonated in my empty chest when I remembered Maria was waiting for an answer.

My dismay met her excited gaze. I turned back and leaned over the paper. What could I say? Anger, disappointment, and betrayal: for what? What did I expect? Nico in shining armor to declare his love for tomboy Lee? He could have at least mentioned something. And why would Maria ask *me* for advice? Did she notice my reaction, my hesitation? Why did I have this reaction and hesitation in the first place? Why didn't anyone like *me*? I did not want Nico and Maria to be together. Humiliation boiled within me.

I wrote back, "Why are you asking me?"

The note returned much quicker than I had hoped. "Because you're his friend… and because I trust you. You seem sensible. I don't want Claudia to be jealous. PLEASE DON'T SAY ANYTHING! So?"

Poor Maria, if only she had known. I sighed. She was the best student in our class, all As, up to par with Evil Centi except that she was not evil at all. I sighed again. This was not my decision to make. These things did not happen to me, only to Viola and girly girls like Maria. I stashed my feelings in the deep hollow where my heart had been and replied, "If you still like him, go for it!"

No one ever wanted *me* as their girlfriend: not Flavio, not Nico, not Peo, despite Nico's insinuations. I thought about some kick-ass women in my vast TV education: the blonde instructor in *Top Gun*, Fujiko chased by Lupin, Aika in love with Rei in *Good morning Spank*, Mila, and even Candy Candy, whom I detested. Most of them were neither nuns nor easy but had admirers and at least one boyfriend.

Me: nothing, zero, the desert.

The note did not come back, but I noticed furtive mail exchanges traveling behind me.

"Balni," Prof. Faramanti startled me. "Sorry to bother you," she said. "Did you do your homework?"

"Hem, sure," I lied.

"Great. What's your answer to problem nine?"

I pretended to search an answer that did not exist in my notebook, but Prof. Faramanti had no patience. "Balni, did you do your homework, or not?"

"Ah, yes, it was right here…" I stammered.

She tromped toward my desk and snatched the notebook from my hand, flipping through the pages. She lost it so fast I didn't have time to brace.

Prof. Faramanti yelled, "No kidding! This

notebook is a *mess*! Either you are lying or even *you* can't find your own work. I don't know which option is more *pitiful*." She tried to rip my notebook to pieces, but it was too thick. Her left eye twitched.

"But I—"

"AND YOU DARE REPLY? OUT! OUT OF MY CLASS, RIGHT NOW!"

Is it true that when you die you leave your body? I must have been close, because I saw myself standing up, trembling, focusing all my might on not crying on my way outside the classroom. She slammed the door after me.

Alone in the hall of shame, I cried.

The order of reprimands in school was: being yelled at, note to the parents, being kicked out of class, Principal's office, and suspension.

Only Nico got himself kicked out of class and for much graver reasons than not doing his homework. I tried to collect myself so it wouldn't be obvious I had cried when the witch called me back in, but she didn't. Rude students would be ousted for ten minutes at most, yet nobody came to get me. Forty-five minutes later the bell rang and Faramanti walked outside.

"Balni," she said without looking at me. Oh, God, this was not over yet. I closed my eyes and tightened my fists waiting for the storm to pass.

"Balni, don't you *ever*, *ever* lie—"

"But—"

"QUIET!" she ordered. "Don't interrupt me! Do yourself a favor and don't speak at all! I did not write a note to your parents because this is between *you* and *me*. Some of your classmates are hopeless, but you are worth my wrath. Do your homework, study hard, and you shall never see it again!"

I opened my mouth like a dead fish, and she stormed away. I *felt* like a dead fish, too.

"Wow," Maria uttered, leaving the class for recess. I hardened my core to prevent an incoming meltdown. Maria added, "Can we get together, sometime?"

I didn't reply. She smiled and left. Nico ambled through the door after her. This time no one would avenge my honor by pissing on a teacher's car. The good old days were gone.

I looked sideways at Nico, approaching diaphanous Maria. She blushed, blue eyes downcast, hidden by her black hair in a pageboy cut. Her ballerina training showed; her limbs were thin and long as if she were one of my paternal Grandma's porcelain figurines. I resented the grace and femininity I didn't have.

Nico leaned on the heater beside her, looking away, arms crossed over his chest. They had nothing in common. Nico and I, instead, shared the things that kept us apart; fear, anger, and resentment.

Well, screw it!

If I cared for no one, no one could hurt me.

Once I came home from the worst school day of my life, Starry asked, putting a piece of toast in front of me, "How did it go?"

"Okay." I was not eager to share the Faramanti fiasco nor my heart problems.

"What did you learn?"

"Stuff." Starry's features collapsed, and she looked at me like a hurt puppy. She had seemed… in the dumps, of late. "What?" I asked, concerned that my unhappiness might be contagious.

"It's just that—" She took a deep breath. "It's pre-puberty, that's what. You're acting like your sister."

What?

I replayed our conversation in my head, seeing her point. I said, "Mom, it's not like that. It's just that… It was boring, that's all."

Her face brightened. "Any new friends?"

I shrugged and forced myself to answer the irritating question. "This girl, Maria, she's nice."

"Would *I* like her?"

"Starry, you would *love* her. Straight As, the best in our class."

"Isn't Evil Centi the best?"

"The *worst,* you mean. They have the same

grades, but she's nice."

"I'm sure he's not that bad either."

"Oh, yeah? He argued that Spartans were right throwing sick kids off a cliff and said it was the *rational* choice. He was looking at Baccellati when he said it, too."

"Oh, boy," Starry conceded. "Well, you should invite Maria over sometime."

"Mm." I pondered on Maria's proposal. Had she taken pity on me after the Faramanti blowout?

"So," Starry changed tone, forcing a strained cheerfulness that announced terrible news.

Oh God, please no more.

She continued, "I would like to move back to Milan."

"*What? Back?* We've never lived in Milan!" I replied.

Starry answered, "*You* have never lived in Milan. I was born and raised there."

"But *why*? Arese is awesome!"

"Arese was okay when you and Viola were children, but now… Viola is in college, you are in middle school, and I'm trapped in this big house by myself all day. It's depressing."

"Oh, and Milan is not? With all that gray and the cars? There are no trees!"

"At least I don't have to drive to get a coffee or the newspaper."

"Like you *do* now. You can make coffee at home

and you *force me* to bike to the newsstand."

Starry huffed. "And see no one?"

"But all my friends are in Arese!"

"And all of mine are in Milan! You just changed school and will make new friends regardless."

"And what about Sonia? And my volleyball team? Grandma? And Fuzzer?"

Starry's nostrils flared and her forehead twitched. She answered, "Grandma will move, too. She has already found a place, Fuzzer will get used to the city and so will you. Listen, I understand it's hard for you, but I know what's best. Believe me."

"Starry, do you?" She balked, and I took the chance to ask something that had been nagging at me since the summer. "Why were you crying by yourself in the kitchen?"

"What? *When*? I wasn't crying."

"Starry, you were! When I came back from vacation, I walked into the kitchen and you were in tears."

She played with her lighter. "Oh, nothing. Who knows? Cutting onions, likely."

I frowned. "Like you ever do. You hate cooking, and you hate onions. You want to know what's going on with me, but you never tell me what's going on with *you*. Even before that, you always told me that everything was fine and then you and Dad split."

She turned back, eyes wide, lips parted. "I… I

wanted to protect you."

"With lies? Well, that didn't work."

When my parents had announced their separation, Dad had left the house within the hour. Again, I was the last one to discover another ineluctable change, our moving. Grandma had already found a place in the big city and I was hearing this for the first time.

With tears welling up in my eyes I asked, "When is this moving thing going to happen?"

Starry's features softened. "Not for a while. We have to sell our house first and then find a place we can afford."

"But our house is *huge*. There is no place that big in Milan!"

Starry laughed. "There are but none we can afford. Real estate is hefty, and half of the profit of selling our house will go to your father. We'll see what we can find."

I huffed. "I hope we can't find anything." Starry smirked, and I continued, "So, why were you crying?"

Starry sighed. "Well, splitting from Dad was... hard. I was so focused on our problems I thought once we split everything would be fine. But it wasn't. When I met Marco—" I cringed. I hated Starry's boyfriend. She continued, "He swept me off my feet, but he, well... Things with him aren't always easy either."

I hadn't seen the hideous boyfriend in a while, but I was so absorbed in my life I hadn't quite noticed. Starry never talked about him because I was no fan.

"Are you fighting?" I asked. As much as I didn't like him, they had been together for several months and it was a done deal.

Starry's face hardened against an impending meltdown, her features twitching. "Sometimes," she confessed, but elaborated no more.

"Dear Jesus, I got your message loud and clear. You sent me the worst day of my life because I was so selfish. I asked you to make *me* happy, but what about everyone else? So, can you please make *everyone* happy?" I imagined the whole planet filled with smiling idiots. "I mean, make everyone happy with a good reason to be happy. If you could do that and have Starry not find a house in Milan while keeping away her evil boyfriend that would be swell. And please let me sleep well with no nightmares. Amen."

I rolled on my side and fell asleep hugging Hairry, the worn out, now tiny sweater that had shared all of my nights.

7

The Ghost

When I came back from school on the following day, Starry loaded me in her Fiat *Panda* car en route to Padua to Viola's rescue.

Hands on the wheel, Starry said, "So, your sister moved in with a ghost."

"Excuse me?"

"Well," she explained puffing on her cigarette. "Her new college friends pulled a prank that worked a little too well. There are weird noises in the house, and after the hoax she's terrified to be alone. Everyone else is away this weekend, and she asked us to go visit."

"Mm," I pondered, uneasy. "And you believe this ghost business?"

"Of course not," Starry answered, behind the

wheel. "You know my opinion on the matter."

"Yeah, I do. Even when your bestie flew on a stool, you thought it was bad digestion. No wonder you didn't believe me when I told you some odd characters lounged around my bed at night."

Starry's smile waned. "How do you know about the seances?"

"Viola told me. Is it true?" I tortured my lower lip.

Starry pursed her mouth in a tight line and then confessed, "Yes."

My stomach lurched. People could levitate on stools. My own mother had seen it happen.

"And you *don't* believe in spirits?" I asked.

Saint Thomas had needed to see to believe but for Starry seeing was not enough.

She answered, "I know what I saw, but what caused it?" She shrugged. "We might have mental abilities that are still mysterious."

"Yep, makes sense. Your friend threatened herself with the glass-and-letter-board trick and then levitated around the room to make the point. I buy it."

Starry rolled her eyes. "Hilarious, Lee. It is also hilarious how the monsters lounging around your bed —or should I call them *odd characters*?—disappeared as you grew up, isn't it?"

Thanks God that was true. I went back to our original topic, "So *why* are we going, if ghosts aren't real?"

Starry bounced in her seat. "To visit! Not only she allowed it but asked me to! I'm concerned about this shack they're living in."

Me too. I was not looking forward to meeting the ghost.

Padua's warm hues of cream, yellow and brown, colored the two to three-story buildings capped by red-tiled roofs. Arched walkways made for elegant sidewalks. It looked much friendlier than Milan, which I found so stark with its oppressive gray skies and architecture.

Viola's directions had us pull over in an alley in front of an ominous building close to the university. The lead sky matched the color of the facade even where painted plaster had collapsed leaving the masonry exposed.

Starry double-checked the address. "Oh, god. This is the place."

The entrance door flung open and Viola burst out, yelling, "Thank god you're here! How are you, guys?"

"Ah well, you?" Starry answered.

"I'm glad to see you!" Viola said hugging herself, frozen on the front steps.

Viola had never been physical and not even a

ghost would change that. My sister had grown into an almost identical copy of Mom: slender, petite, with the typical Italian olive complexion I lacked. She didn't smile often, but when she did her hazel eyes brightened her face. After a brief preppy phase and a longer punk one, she had settled on wearing inside out sweats and ratty, old clothes. She was beautiful nonetheless.

Mom and I dragged our bags into the house. The interior was dark.

Starry suggested, "Ah, you could use more light in here."

Viola huffed. "Starry, let's be clear, this is no palace. We're all broke, okay?"

Starry chewed on her lip. Dad gave her alimony to cover our expenses, but somehow it was never enough.

We dropped our bags in Viola's bedroom.

My sister said, "Lee, I hope you don't mind sleeping on the floor. I have a camping mat and blankets. Starry can sleep in Alessandra's room, but my other roommate, Paola, is particular and doesn't want to share her space."

The hint of kindness in her voice startled me. "Ah, sure. That's fine."

She beamed. "Great! I'm almost done with dinner!"

"*Dinner*?" Starry and I exclaimed at the same time.

"*You* made dinner?" Starry reiterated.

"Yes! Check it out!"

Viola led the way to the kitchen. Cracked tiles covered the floor in spots. The plaster on the wall near the ceiling was stained and moldy.

"And what's on the menu?" Starry scrutinized the pot steaming on the stove. Patches of light yellow enamel matched the peeling cabinets.

"Campbell's soup! Mushroom flavor, okay?"

Viola picked up the plastic spoon she had left in the pot, retrieving only the handle. She darted a furtive glance at Starry, who was checking the view from the window. Unseen by Mom, Viola snuck the stump of the half-melted spoon into the garbage.

Starry mumbled, "Yeah, soup sounds great. Where did you learn to make it?" She did not seem interested in the answer.

Viola rummaged for a new unmelted utensil. "Ah, one of my roommates. It's easy, you add water and warm it up."

I felt like gagging, but did not betray my sister's culinary secrets. If the plastic did not kill me, the grime that covered the orange laminate table would do the job. Starry didn't notice it.

Viola changed the topic. "Any news on the apartment hunt in Milan?"

Since I had to pee as well, I asked, "Ah, Viola, where is the restroom?"

"Out of the kitchen, first door on the left. To flush just empty the bucket of water down the toilet."

Starry and I looked at her, horrified.

"And it works?" I asked.

"Like a charm," my sister reassured me.

"So, what was with the prank?" I asked once Viola, Starry, and I had sat around the table to eat our mushroom-with-melted-utensil soup.

Viola explained, somber, "Irma Piona, the old lady who lived here before us, died in the house—"

"THUMP!"

We jumped. "What was *that*?" Starry asked.

"IRMA! I told you!" Viola whispered, paling.

I scoffed. "Oh, *come on*! It came from outside!" *Who's the scaredy-cat now?*

My sister had spent years tormenting me about my childish fear of monsters, but I held my tongue and she continued, "So, I was being… jumpy on the topic and they shook me up a little. Two days ago I was home by myself—"

"Did you skip class?" Starry interrupted.

"Geez, Starry, no! It's not high school! Anyway, I noticed this strange guy outside my bedroom window, all dressed in black, with a balaclava of all things, and a red umbrella. Weird, right?"

"Yeah, that's weird," Starry commented, and I agreed. Nobody wore a balaclava in Italy, especially in October.

"THUMP!"

"Did you hear *now*?" Viola asked.

"Yeah, fine. It's an old house, chill," I answered.

Viola took a deep breath. "Anyway, I closed the shutters. The phone rang, then stopped, then it rang again. I picked up, but no one was on the other side. Meanwhile, I noticed that the umbrella guy had moved. I could see him outside of the kitchen window, closer this time."

"*Merda*!" I exclaimed, and Starry hit me on the head.

Viola carried on, "Right? I ran to lock all the doors. The phone rang again then stopped. That's when the odd, rapping sound started, like a mouse, or better like two fingers scratching on the door. It came from the closet in the entrance. I mustered my courage and opened it. Irma Piona was staring at me, she had hung herself in the freaking closet," Viola's voice wavered. I almost had a heart attack.

"*What*?" Starry and I exclaimed, at once.

"Well, it wasn't her. It was Alessandra. And the guy with the umbrella was my friend Boga. And Paola was the one on the phone. But I screamed so loud and freaked out so much that… Well, let's say I fell for it."

I sympathized with my poor sister.

"THUMP!"

This time I jumped, too. We turned toward the wall that separated the kitchen from the bathroom and the cabinet doors flew open.

What do you do when you witness the impossible with your own eyes? Was the house haunted? In our general bewilderment the cabinet flung a glass at us.

What the CAZZO?

My jaw dropped as a plastic juicer flew off the shelf toward the table where we were still sitting, dumbstruck. When a glass followed, the three of us stood.

Viola screeched, running for cover, but Starry stalked to the cabinet, which flung a teapot at her. It hit her square on the head.

"SON OF A—" Starry crouched in pain.

"Oh, God, Starry, are you okay?" I asked trying not to laugh, because the situation was surreal, scary and comical, and Starry *never* swore.

Viola remained behind the table, which was wise given the good aim of old Irma's ghost.

My sister mumbled, wide-eyed, "How in the world?"

Starry stood up, holding her forehead with one hand and slamming the cantankerous cabinet closed with the other. It was the last straw. The whole wall collapsed in a massive rumble of plaster.

Starry jumped back, covering her face with her arms. When calm settled again, she looked like the ghost of Irma Piona herself, aghast and covered in white dust.

The kitchen was in shambles as we stared at the bathroom sink on the other side of the rubble that had been the wall.

Silence didn't last too long.

As Viola and I realized that the poltergeist phenomenon was due to the rotten wall succumbing to gravity and the cabinets slanting forward as a consequence, we both exploded in hysterical laughter.

Starry yelled, "Are you *crazy*? I could have *died*!" But she was alive, and the more she looked at us, fuming and covered in plaster, the louder we laughed. She trailed off, giving in to hysterics, too.

Nothing is bonding like intense fear followed by relief and uncontrollable laughter. Perhaps that's why Americans have a tradition of telling horror stories around a campfire. Italians, or at least my family, opted to squat in a derelict, crumbling building, instead.

That night, when we turned off the light, the familiar sound of my sister rocking back and forth in her bed brought a smile to my lips. She was listening to her Walkman. She had done it to escape awful nightmares as a child… worse than mine, and the habit had stuck.

The noise stopped.

"Did you hear?" she asked.

"What? I wouldn't worry about it, it's an old house. Not like the kitchen wall just crumbled."

Viola chuckled. "Wow, you grew up, Lee."

I tried not to preen in her much-awaited compliment. "About time, I guess, right?"

We both snickered. I didn't want our conversation to end.

Vanna, the owner of the shack, had sent a friend to inspect the house, which was deemed safe enough for Viola and her friends to keep squatting. The kitchen wall, not structural, had caved in due to a water leak, which explained why the toilet didn't work. Starry had threatened to force Viola out of the place, but my big sister had just shrugged, ignoring her.

My most treasured times with Viola were our wee-hour conversations in the few nights we had shared on vacation. Sometimes drama or loneliness pushed my sister to unseal her tight shell, and I was hoping for one of those rare moments.

"So, are you still dating Renzo?" I asked.

Over a year earlier, she had fallen for the much older light-technician while vacationing at the seaside. In spite of the odds, Dad's wrath, and a few misadventures, they had ended up together. Their story had made me believe I had to wish harder to get my own happy ending.

"Nope," Viola answered.

"Oh, I'm sorry! He was cool," I said, surprised at her lack of heartache. Dad had predicted that Renzo would move on to the next young fool in no time.

Mischief oozed from Viola's voice as she answered, "Yeah, he was cute, but not as cute as Volker! So I dumped Renzo."

"Wait, *what*?" I ran a mental list of Viola's favorite rock stars but came up empty-handed. *Volker?*

She turned on her side, sounding excited. "Promise to say nothing?"

"Of course!"

"Well, remember when I went to the seaside in Liguria, last summer, with Marta and her parents?"

"Yes." Viola and her bestie had taken a break after enduring the harsh maturity exam that ended high school.

"Well, *I didn't*!" Viola bantered, testing my reaction.

"*What*?"

"Well I did, but Marta's parents were not in the picture. It was only the two of us."

"Wow! Total freedom! That's awesome and

insane! How did you get away with it?"

"Well, I told Starry that Marta's parents were there. They had no idea, but were cool about us going solo. You know, it's not like they care. Anyway, one night these two guys followed us on a stroll along the beach, and we pretended to be German not to be harassed."

"I thought your German wasn't too hot," I commented.

"It's not, and the guys turned out to be German for real. We laughed so hard. Anyway, that's how I met Volker. He's the spit image of Martin Kemp, the bass player of Spandau Ballet."

As if I could ignore Martin Kemp after living with my sister for years.

"So, he's your new *beau*?" I asked.

"Yep."

"And how do you communicate?"

"In English, more or less. He learned some Italian."

"Does he live in Liguria?"

"No, he lives in Germany, but he should come visit soon. I can't wait!"

"Well, I'm happy for you. How old is he?"

"Twenty-two." Older than Viola, but not ten years, like Renzo.

My sister resumed her rocking back and forth, listening to music, and I wondered how love could be so whimsical. Viola had risked disownment for

Renzo the light-technician and yet, he was history. The old guy had ended up with a broken heart. Ha. Dad could be wrong, after all.

8

Boobless Bras

On Sunday, once back from Padua, I rang Sonia's doorbell with a heavy heart.

"Yeeees?" Sonia's Mom answered in her characteristic slow drawl, adjusting the glasses on her nose and squinting.

"*Buongiorno*, Mrs. Rosati. Is Sonia at home?"

"Yes, but she has to study."

"Moooooom!" Sonia's voice startled the small lady. My very tall friend emerged from behind her. "Yo, Lee, come in!"

"Ah, but I…" I looked at her mother, who turned to protest toward Sonia.

"Sonia, you *have to* study!" she asserted again, her voice modulating her characteristic whiny tone.

"Yeah, yeah, yeah."

Sonia buzzed the gate open. Embarrassed, I walked in. Her mom threw her hands in the air in frustration and left.

I asked, "Ah, is *that* okay?"

Sonia rolled her eyes. "Yeah, don't worry. She's *always* like that, no matter what I do. So I stopped caring."

"Wow." Starry would have grounded me for much less.

"Where the heck have you been yesterday?" she asked.

"To visit my sister. I have to catch you up on some—"

"Yeah, yeah, yeah…"

Sonia waved me off and we entered her little bedroom. A copy of *Cioè* lay open on the bed. *Cioè*, which more or less translates as *actually*, had become a fad, one of those words kids said in place of pauses. It was a very appropriate title for the magazine that talked about everything *normal* girls were interested in and that should have been instead a dignified silence.

I sat on the mattress, leafing through *Cioè*. "So, why do you like this so much?"

"Are you kidding me? You've never read it?"

"Ah, Mom forbids it," I admitted. Was it me or her who thought the magazine stupid?

"Oh, wow! It's about everything that matters! See? Tom Cruise, Duran Duran, but the best part is the mail."

Sonia joined me on the bed and read out loud, "Dear Cioè, I am desperate. I don't know who else to ask for help. If I use tampons, do I lose my virginity?"

We both laughed. Then I asked, "What's a tampon?"

"I have no idea! Isn't this great? It's all about sex and stuff. Check it out!"

I was used to Starry knowing right away when something was wrong, but that was not the case with Sonia. Rather than reading the silly mag, I stated, "I might move."

"What? And where are you going?" she asked, unfazed, turning a page.

"Milan."

"For sure?"

"It seems like it."

"And you don't want to?"

"Of course not, Sonia! The city stinks! And what about you, the volleyball team, and everything else?"

Sonia admired a two-pager full bleed picture of Tom Cruise and said, "I moved from Rome, and it was all right. I made new friends, I met you."

"Wouldn't you *miss me*?" I asked, appalled.

"Yeah, but you wouldn't be *that* far. Plus, cities are awesome. I loved Rome."

She sighed, and I thought the news had sunk in.

"What?" I asked.

"Nothing." She sighed again, and then added, "It's just that all these hot hunks make me miss Ermanno even more."

"*Who*?"

"Ermanno, my boyfriend."

"You have a *boyfriend*?"

"Are you *surprised*?" Sonia asked.

"Ah, no," I lied. "How come I never met him? And do your parents know?"

"Of course not! They would kill me! I met him last summer at the seaside, in Ostia. He's *so* hot!"

My jaw went slack. "Wow. Did you *kiss* him?"

"Not yet. I am not sure he knows he's my boyfriend. He's thirteen. But I'll make that clear next year." She winked, and we both laughed. Then she asked, "What about you?"

"*What*?" My mood dampened again.

"Do you have someone you like?"

I cringed thinking about Nico leaning on the heater beside Maria. Perhaps Sonia had a piece of advice I could use to win the darn thug back.

I let out a long, sad sigh. "Sonia, I don't know. There's this kid at school I might like. He's a screwup, but we've always been friends."

"Is he hot?"

I smirked. "Oh yeah, as hot as hell."

Sonia bounced on the bed. "Tell me more, tell me more!"

"There's nothing else to say. He asked a classmate of mine to *be together.*"

"Ouch, that sucks."

"Yeah, I guess. Sonia, are you sure you like Ermanno?"

"What's there not to like? He's hot, green eyes and all."

Her answer perplexed me. I said, "Well, it doesn't matter anyway if I like him or not. He's taken."

"Right, right. Find another one, the world is full. Look! Duran Duran pictures!"

"It's not *that* simple! What if he's *the one*?"

Sonia rolled her eyes. "Geez, Lee! You're so dramatic! You aren't even sure if you like him! Just tell him and see what happens."

"*Are you out of your mind?*"

"*You* are! It is *that simple*! You like complicated things but this is not one of them. You like him, yes or no? If yes, ask him. Either you end up together, or you move on."

I didn't answer, hurt by my friend's bluntness. She didn't notice, and soon I forgot, too.

It was the dead of November. The sky, gray for weeks, melted into an incessant rain that soaked everything with tedium. Rotten chill insinuated itself between skin and bones like mold, drenching my soul with unhappiness.

I would have much rather done without phys ed to be at the pool for a month. I couldn't stand swimming laps, and I already had to go twice a week to straighten my nerdy back, bent by too many novels.

My sadist, out-of-school trainer craved my pain without being able to see it. His fierce lessons had turned me into a competitive swimmer in spite of my disinterest. I loved the water, but only in summer, when I could snorkel, dive, and frolic.

My flip-flops slapped against the wet tiles and I dropped my towel on the bench by the pool.

"Boobs, boobs, *boobs*!" Nico uttered ahead of me, staring at Veronica the Airhead's bodacious forms and startling me out of my musings. He didn't even said hi.

I sighed, commiserating my flat chest, then noticed Maria's demoralized expression. I wondered how things were going between Nico and her. After the day he had *asked* her, I had not seen them together much.

Chlorine stung my nostrils. I stared outside the pool fogged up windows. The clouded sky looked like blurred lead, even through the neon light scattered around by the thick, humid air. The pool shimmered, and I decided it was a dream. I would wake up in Sardinia as soon as I touched the cold water.

I didn't.

Back and forth, lap after lap, the gurgle of each stroke alternated with the cries and echoes of my classmates, dilating in the steam. After a while, I noticed Baccellati, forlorn, standing outside the pool, fully clothed.

"Hey, Baccellati, no swimming for you?"

"Ah!" he uttered. A hint of a black mustache darkened his upper lip, above his big front teeth. I wondered if he had gotten his first MEN-struation.

Since I stared at him, he answered, "I have to guard everyone's flip-flops."

His strange accent was different from Sonia's or Nico's. I guessed he was also from the south of Italy, but some other region. His eyes were transfixed on the pile of plastic slippers by the edge of the pool.

"Ah, I see. But why *you*? Don't you want to swim?"

"*No*!" he replied fast. His eyes, glued to the flip-flops, widened. "My parents say it's *dangerous*. You can get warts and stuff."

True story. I still remembered how painful it had been to remove the two on my left heel.

He continued, "… And they say I have to guard everyone's shoes, or someone will steal them."

"Ah, well, thank you?"

Baccellati flashed me a huge smile that reflected

the light emanating from the ceiling on his big front teeth.

The theft of slippers was unlikely, but the risk of warts was monstrously tangible. I swam and thought of Baccellati, dejected by the pool, soaking in the muggy, artificial light, the chlorine smell stuck to his skin and hair. Removing warts had been the most painful event of my life, yet I thought it preferable to the slow and consuming public humiliation of not even taking a chance.

Once in the locker room, I got out of the shower, and Maria startled me. "Can I talk to you?"

"Ah, sure." I towel-dried my hair, and we walked toward the back of the locker room. She chose a corner that ensured privacy thanks to the loud blow-dryers.

"What's up?" I prodded.

"Well… Things with Nico aren't great," she answered.

My heart did a little dance, but then I saw her eyes and soaked up her sadness. "I'm sorry to hear. What's wrong?"

She mussed her wet hair. "I don't know. I guess nothing's wrong, but nothing's happening either."

"Like *what*?"

She shrugged, sitting on a wooden bench.

Droplets fell to her shoulders, darkening her pink t-shirt. "He ignores me," she said. "He keeps looking at the other girls. I have no idea why he asked *me*."

"Did you kiss?" Maria shook her head. I added, "That's strange."

Nico had kissed his share of girls, no doubt. I had no claim over him, yet tension released my shoulders.

Maria's big blue eyes lifted to meet mine. "Right? Should I break up with him?"

Yes! Yes! Mr. Hyde screamed in my head, but I ignored him asking instead, "Do you still like him?"

"Yeah."

I sighed, strangling Mr. Hyde. "Then why break up with him? I mean, he's not shy, but if he likes you for real… Maybe *that* makes him shy."

She paused then asked, "Should I talk to him?"

"Why not? As a couple that's the least you can do." I winked, and she shoved me aside, a big smile back on her delicate face.

As we walked to the blow-dryers, I asked, "So, are you still up for doing homework together, sometime?"

Maria beamed at me. "I would love to!"

Really?

"Fine," Blondie conceded appearing behind us, oblivious to the fact she had not been part of the conversation.

"When?" asked Claudia, Maria's freckled best friend, popping out of a changing room.

I hadn't meant this to be a group invitation, yet the Three Marys, as Prof. Visoni called Maria and her two friends, were inseparable. The nickname was biblical in nature, something to do with Jesus, but we all knew the *Tre Marie*, the Three Marys, as a brand of *Colomba* and *Panettone*, the typical desserts for Easter and Christmas.

Oh, well. The more, the merrier, like Dad said all the time. I proposed, "This afternoon?"

"Sounds good!" the Three Marys answered.

Big news was on the horizon.

That afternoon, when the Three Marys came over, I was nervous. Starry instead was delighted that I hang out with *girls*, some of them with good grades, too. She was not a huge fan of Sonia.

The Three Marys and I sprawled on my tiny bedroom's floor to do homework.

"How come you're so good with math problems, Lee? You make it look like you never study," Maria flattered me.

"I do?"

"Good thing she sucks in Geography," Blondie remarked. "I saw you cheating on the test, way back."

Everyone stared at me.

"I tried," I confessed, recounting the real story and how I kept getting very undeserved grades in spite of my unsurmountable ignorance of Visoni's subject. I swallowed, waiting for the girls' reaction.

"Wow," Claudia said. "You got spunk, *girl*!" She gave me a high five.

Nobody had ever called me *girl* before, and the weirdest thing was that I liked it.

The afternoon flew by. The more we were honest with each other, the more our trust grew. Topics became more personal and private.

"By the way," Claudia said. I stopped and looked at her. "No, nothing." She turned purple and resumed writing.

"What?" I asked, and everyone else prodded her, elbowing and encouraging her.

"Fine! It's… weird. Ah, do any of you have, like a bruise on your chest?"

"I do!" I exclaimed. I assumed I had rammed into something. "You too?" Claudia nodded. "How come?"

"I thought —I don't know— what if our boobs are growing?"

"Wow, with bruises? God really didn't care for girls." I touched my sore, flat chest. "But I hope that's the case."

If I didn't grow some, I had no place in the world. A shark had eaten the only flat-chested woman in *Baywatch* within a few episodes.

Maria blushed in turn. "Do you guys have, well, any hair down there?"

"*You do*?" Claudia blurted.

Maria laughed so hard she startled us. "Yes, yes I do, but… oh, God, it's so funny."

"What is?" I asked, jealous.

She pulled her lips in a tight line, then said, "I have three long hairs, that's all."

We exploded in laughter. Puberty was on its way.

Once we finished our homework, we wandered into Starry's closet. It was huge. Since Dad had moved out she had taken over his closet as well, so now she had two, huge walk-in closets: winter and summer.

"Are you sure it's okay?" Maria asked, biting her lip.

"Why not?" I opened Starry's drawers, one at the time. "Here it is!" I laid my eyes on Starry's underwear.

"Score! What size is she?" Claudia asked.

"What sizes are there?" I asked.

Blondie explained, "First size if you're flat, second if you're small, third big boobs, all the way up to sixth: that's ridiculous boobs."

I wanted to make sure I understood. "So,

Veronica has a sixth?"

I wondered if her upbringing on Barbie dolls had caused her *hormones* to kick in early. Mine, at least judging by my flat chest, were dormant or missing. Prof. Faramanti would have been proud of my *hypothesis*.

"No," Claudia answered. "I asked, she has a third."

"WOW! Sixth is a lot of boobs. Third too. My Mom must be first or second."

"Perfect!" Maria said. "Check her size."

I turned around one of her bras. "It's a first, yay! *Oh, my*! Look at this one, it's so cute."

Among many lacy and gross adult-looking bras, I found a white cotton tank top with green polka dots.

"Nice!" The Three Marys buzzed. "Try it on, try it!"

We spent at least an hour taking turns trying the huge top. To make it somewhat fit, one of us pulled the back tight, so it adhered to our flat chests. We had a blast. Girls were not so bad, even Blondie.

When everyone packed up to leave, Maria seized my wrist and whispered, "Nico and I broke up." Her blue eyes were shimmery and sad.

"NO! What happened?" I blurted amidst very mixed feelings.

She wrung her hands, staring at them. "We

talked at recess, but what could I say? I didn't want to sound clingy, right?" We nodded, and she continued, "I was so embarrassed, and he just looked bored. It was awful. I thought if I broke up with him he would wake up, do something, be upset. But he shrugged and walked away."

"What a *stronzo*." I hadn't talked to him much since they had gotten together, and I wondered what the hell was going on in his rotten head. "I'm sorry."

Maria replied, "Whatever. He obviously didn't care."

I was about to find out.

9

Out with a bang

On a Saturday at recess I doodled on my planner. Viola had told me that in some countries kids stayed at home on Sunday *and* on Saturday. It seemed like a great idea.

After her initial upset at discovering my rampage in her underwear, Starry gifted me the polka dot bra, moved by the much-anticipated beginning of my puberty. The pediatrician said my boobs could take years to grow, and I should expect my first period at thirteen, the average between my mom's and sister's menarche. I was confident he had been kidding.

Romeo startled me by asking with a malicious grin, "So, did you hear about the breakup?"

I jumped in my chair due to my uncanny ability

to zonk out of existence while drawing.

"Yep," I answered, careful to hide my relief.

"And…?"

I looked at Romeo's face, round like that of an angel, brown hair falling on his forehead, and I replied, "What do you mean? I couldn't care less. How's Nico instead?"

"He couldn't care less either."

"Yeah, right. Boys never hurt, do they? You're too cool to care."

He frowned. "No, he *really* didn't care. You promise not to tell Vani?" Vani was Maria's last name.

"Okay." Curiosity prevented me to pull back.

"Nico bragged that he overheard Vani in the locker room saying she had a crush on him. We bet. He asked her and she said yes. That jerk cost me one thousand liras."

"You *bet* on Maria?" My outrage washed over Romeo like a tsunami.

"Easy, easy! No harm done. That goof didn't even make out! In his place—"

"Spare me." I left him at my desk, tromping straight to Nico.

His black hair fell over his brown eyes. He smiled, then saw my treacherous look and tilted his head sideways as if to hear something better.

"Nico," I dropped my voice to an angry whisper. "You *bet* on Maria?"

He rolled his eyes and his face hardened. “None of your freaking business, Balni.”

His comment burned. “You’re my friend, and I thought you weren’t a jerk.”

“Well, you were *wrong*. Didn’t you get the memo? Get over it.”

“I can’t. I know better. You might have hurt her! Why would you ask her if you didn’t care?”

“Better Vani than a nun like you!” he said, as bitter as he could manage, which was very bitter indeed.

The jab pierced me like an ice dagger. I turned around and walked away to hide the tears in my eyes.

“Dear Jesus, you were right. Nico *is* a jerk and I will never talk to him again. Please make him sorry. Very, very sorry. Keep him awake, send him nightmares, whatever is best. I wouldn’t hope in redemption but some guilt if we're lucky. And please make everyone happy with good reason, except Nico, and let me sleep well with no nightmares. Amen.”

I ignored Nico for days. I wondered if he didn’t

care, didn't notice, or if he was angry, too. The Italian teacher gave us back our compositions: A-.

Ha, that's a first.

I loved writing. Did my bad mood seep into my words?

At recess Nico came by my desk where I was intent on a new art-piece: drawing my name graffiti-style on the page where my homework assignments should have been. I pretended not to see him.

"Didn't get an A?" Nico asked, leaning on the desk in front of mine.

How the hell…?

"Scram," I uttered.

Since he didn't move nor flinch, but stared at me with his arms crossed over his chest, I stood up to leave.

"Balni!" His voice sounded hurt, so I turned, surprised.

I had concluded that Nico had no feelings, but I was hoping to find out I was wrong. It terrified me he might humiliate me again, or crush me with one of his insensitive remarks. We had been playing this tiresome game for years. I turned. He looked at me, eyes wide, lips parted, but did not say a thing. I took a step away from him.

He slammed a fist on a desk. "What the hell is *your* problem?" he said.

"*This* is my problem, Nico. You act like an ass

and you hurt people on purpose, and I don't like it."

"I hurt *you*?" His eyes went wide. I shrugged. "When?" His voice was shrill.

"When you called me a nun and when you acted like a *stronzo*… like now."

"I didn't… Geez, Lee, I didn't mean to *hurt* you, I… You're going all girl on me and I… *Al diavolo*! I don't know what I'm doing, okay?"

"What do you mean?" I blurted. Did he care? He had even called me Lee, which hadn't happened in a long time.

Nico explained, "Well, things were just starting to make sense and then this love stuff came into the picture. Or hormones, or both. Anyway, nothing makes sense anymore. The Vani business didn't seem like a big deal, and she didn't seem to care either and I… *Merda*, Lee, you *are* a nun!"

I stared at him, shocked, throughout his rant. The only thing that stuck was that he had been listening when Prof. Faramanti had spoken about hormones and, most of all, that he really thought I was *a nun*. The whole speech sounded like an attempted apology, failed.

I fought tears. "What the hell does that even mean?"

He seemed as flustered as I was. "That you don't like anyone, *ever*!"

Right. I *hated* him. Maybe. I asked, outraged,

"What do you know about whom I like?"

"Well, Peo's been after you for years. You don't even talk to him."

"You're making stuff up! Peo and I are *friends*!"

"I told you he had a crush on you, and you kept ignoring him."

"He does *not*! I did not!"

He threw his hands up in the air. "Come here for Christ's sake."

Everyone else was out in the hallway and it was only the two of us in the classroom. I had no idea where he was going with any of this. I trudged toward him in spite of my rushing heartbeat, torturing a cuticle on my thumb.

He murmured, "Closer. Look here." Just being close to him bothered me. Maybe because I was so darn angry.

I examined the pencil case he had seized from a desk, full of writings and names. It reminded me of the graffiti wall outside our old elementary school. I followed Nico's finger to a big heart with my name inside: *Leda*.

I stepped back, bewildered, and Nico smirked. "See? I didn't lie. This is Peo's."

"I, um, what am I supposed to do?"

He shrugged, his smirk gone. "You ask *me*? I have no clue with this *merda*. I'm doing everything wrong, *apparently*." He paused, looking at me, then sighed. "Talk to him. Spend time with him, I guess.

What the *cazzo* do I know?" He looked away.

"But… I don't like him that way," I confessed. Peo was a brother to me.

A smile cracked Nico's face. "You *don't*? See what I mean when I say you're *a nun*? What is there not to like? He's a great guy. Heart of gold, good lookin'. I didn't want to offend you, but geez, you just don't care. Do you?"

"*What*?" I answered, shell-shocked. I thought *he* didn't care. And yes, Peo *was* awesome, yet still a friend.

Nico continued, "And don't give me that *merda, I don't hurt people on purpose*," he imitated my angry voice, "because sometimes you have to, like walking away from Peo, and other times you choose to, like avoiding me for days." He gave me an accusatory stare.

I. Was. Speechless. Did Nico the Thug just tell me off? Did he admit that by avoiding him I had hurt him? Did I hurt Peo? I was still staring at him mouth agape.

He tilted his head sideways, in his characteristic way. "Are we cool?"

I nodded, and he walked away.

With my feelings in a jumble, I felt everything but cool.

Days blurred into weeks. It was hard to keep track when every day looked dark and gray, but when Christmas lights went up my mood had used to switch. Now I hated Holidays, split in between Mom and Dad, whom I saw for dinner on Christmas Day in Grandma Magda's kingdom of doilies and untouchable porcelain trinkets.

Dad proposed that we spend more time together by joining his friends skiing in the Alps for one week, in mid-December. Teachers hadn't been crazy about me missing school days, but they let it slide.

On the departure day, Dad picked me up in his brand-new, forest-green Audi 90 ten minutes earlier than planned.

"What about your friends?" I asked in between fear and curiosity.

"We'll meet them there. You'll see, they're nice."

I was wearing skinny jeans, as dictated by the current fashion, with a *fuchsia* sweater. I detested pink, and Starry knew it, yet she kept buying me pink clothes in the hope I would wake up a princess, one day.

Nonetheless I had worn the fuchsia knit, since it brought out my green eyes, and it was definitely *not* nun material. Was I *trying* to be pretty? I wondered if Nico had noticed. We had spoken little after our odd exchange two weeks earlier.

While heading north it started snowing. *So lovely.*

Dad cursed in his peculiar, non vulgar way, "Son of a witch!"

"At least there will be plenty on the slopes," I joked to ease his mood.

"True. I'd rather do without it on the road, though."

I could see his point. The snow accumulated and visibility decreased lengthening our journey to Bormio.

A truck moved to our central lane to pass a *Panda* car and Dad hit the brakes. The Audi slid sideways giving me a thrill, "Slippery, huh?" I joked.

And then everything went black.

I opened my eyes, confused and covered with shattered glass. I tried to lift my right hand to my face, but my arm was stuck. Panicked, I looked down at the mangled plastic and twisted metal trapping me against my seat: my side of the car had rammed into a big tree.

Nothing hurt. I snapped my head left, looking for Dad. He was not in his seat. The windshield had cracked, but not shattered. Dad's door opened onto a field. The cars on the highway zipped by in the rear-view mirror.

Dad stood in the emergency lane, pacing back and forth in the snow, muttering to himself.

"Dad! Daaaad!" I called, terrified and angry.

Is he in shock? Did he leave without checking with me first? Is the car going to explode like in the movies?

As soon as he heard me, Dad ran like a madman toward me. "Chunky! Chunky! Are you okay?"

He reserved the nickname Chunky for his rare, sweetest moments. It was endearing only because I was skinny.

"Ah, I have no idea," I answered. "What happened?"

He looked at me bewildered. "*You don't remember*? I think you're in shock."

Apparently we had been in a car accident and Dad, after making sure I was all right and the car was safe, had gone to the emergency phone to call for help. The vehicle was a wreck, and the truck was on its way.

If the tree had hit us a centimeter closer, I would have been dead. I thanked Jesus under my breath. He did not make me happy with good reason, but at least he kept me alive. Funny how the second trumped the first, yet it had never occurred to me to ask Jesus to do just that. Maybe I had gotten greedy over the years, taking things for granted.

Dad helped me, and a car pulled over. I shivered, and I recovered my ski jacket from the wreckage. I snuggled into it.

"Carloooo! Carloooo!" A redhead ran out of the Golf that had just stopped in the emergency lane.

What the hell?

"Vera!" Dad called back, relief flooding his face. She ran to hug Dad, who reassured her. "We're fine, we're fine." He summarized our ordeal as I walked up to them. Dad saw me from the corner of his eye and said, "Vera, this is Leda. Lee, this is my friend, Vera."

"Nice to meet you," I said shaking her hand. She was around Dad's age, with gorgeous hazel eyes, plenty of freckles and a sweet, genuine smile. I liked her.

She offered to take me to the hotel while Dad waited for the truck.

Swearing, head-first into Vera's trunk, Dad tried to cram in our luggage. Some of it ended up strapped to the ski-rack on the roof.

Within twenty minutes I found myself in the back seat, squeezed between two kids and a bunch of baggage on our way to Bormio. Alessio, blond, sturdy and with a big smile, was Vera's son, two years my elder. He had an evil sister seven years older, just like me. His little cousin, on my other side, was dark haired and did not talk.

A sudden, loud bang interrupted the conversation. I gripped the seats in front of me fearing for my life. *Twice in a day? Impossible*! I shut my eyes as tight as I could, hoping to wake. When I opened them we were once again in the emergency lane.

"What the hell?" Vera exhaled, gritting her teeth, hands squeezing the wheel.

Alessio turned to check behind us. "I think we lost our roof-luggage!"

A car came up, lighting up the luggage and swerving to avoid it last minute, honking.

"Devils!" Vera cursed under her breath. "If something happens you, Alessio, walk to the closest emergency phone and call Uncle, understood? I'm gonna get the darn suitcase," Vera stated with the strongest resolve ever.

She walked out in the snow, ran across the highway, and came back with the luggage.

Wow, what a woman!

She threw the suitcase on top of what was on our laps, and we resumed our journey. Dad sure had cool friends.

When we reached our destination, I marveled at Bormio, quiet under a blanket of fresh snow. The buildings with wooden balconies and shutters looked like gingerbread homes, icicles dripping from the aged slate roofs. The Alps seemed so close you felt you could touch them, enormous giants overlooking the villages scattered in the valley.

Dad joined us for dinner, somber; his new car was totaled. My minor concussion was nothing that a good polenta with mushrooms couldn't cure.

When I got back home, one week later, Starry asked, hugging me full force, "How did it go?"

"Awesome!"

"In spite of the accident?"

"Yes, like I told you, and it happened ages ago."

"It was only a week ago."

"Right, ages."

"And what's *that*?" she screamed, gaping at my neck.

"Oh, *that*, nothing. Just a scab from the seatbelt." I showed off my war wound with pride.

Teary-eyed, Mom hugged me tight. I didn't mind one bit. I sure said goodbye to 1989 with a bang. 1990, one of the best years of my life, was about to bring some big surprises.

PART 2

10

The Company

Spring rushed along, shoved away by an early summer. At the beginning of June Arese's middle school kids took part in the *Super Tournament*, a sports competition where boys challenged each other at soccer and girls at volleyball.

We would face only other first-year teams. The massive participation was due to the fact that the games happened at night at the oratory, the playground run by the church. This meant kids went out, without parents, for several hours every weeknight for a whole week with the excuse of either playing or cheering somebody else.

I was the captain of our volleyball team. After one year of practicing with Sonia in the oratory's team I was a strong player, in spite of my height.

The night of our first and hopefully not last game, I locked my bike and noticed Nico.

"Hey," I greeted him. "Here to cheer us?"

"More like to watch Laura's *culo* in her shorts."

Why do I bother? "Dude, she's your best friend's girl," I reminded him.

Laura and Romeo had been dating for a month, and it seemed serious.

"Hey, I'm just watching." Nico smirked joining the other guys from our class: Peo, Romeo, Baccellati, and even Evil Centi.

Evil Centi was an enigmatic kid: smart to the point of making me uncomfortable and, instead of being a nerd, athletic, too. Unfortunately, he was mean, really mean. I was witnessing the childhood of the next great villain, because I had no doubt that he would make the memory of Hitler fade, one day.

"*What?*" Evil Centi glared at me with those incredible gray eyes of his.

"You've got something on your face," I lied, startled.

"Yeah, Balni, it's called genius. You wouldn't recognize it if it came with a manual."

"No, Centi, I'm pretty sure it's bird shit," I answered, walking away and taking in with the corner of my eye his panicked reaction.

Nico leaned over the metal barricade that surrounded the volleyball court. After his breakup with Maria he had stayed single as far as I knew.

I stepped onto the outdoor court, bright lights making me nervous. We were playing against a class from the other middle school in Arese, Col Di Lana, our same section, therefore, our archenemies. 1A versus 1A, like a *derby*, when two soccer teams from the same city faced each other: Milan A.C. vs. International, Lazio vs. Roma, Juventus vs. Torino. In short, it was a big deal.

The referee called the captains to shake hands, and I found myself face to face with Lexi, a tall girl from my *real* volleyball team: our middle blocker. *Merda.* Our setter, Sara, was at her side. They were strong, even more so together.

Lexi smirked. "Hey Lee, you don't stand a chance."

"We shall see," I answered, holding up her gaze.

We lost fifteen to three in the most miserable game in history.

When I left the court, Nico walked toward me. "Good game, Lee."

I glared at his handsome face. "Are you making fun of us?"

"Not of you. You did great. Veronica lost for everyone."

"It's a *team sport*! If you hadn't insulted her

throughout the game, she would have done better!"

Could I ever, for once, talk to Nico without verbally assaulting him? Apparently not.

He rolled his eyes and walked away. Our friendship had degraded to bitter bickering all the time. Why? My slippery bike lock resisted my fumbling. Nico had the power to hurt me, and I attacked him first to prevent that from happening.

I was so used to my family that not being loved by everyone else was a scary thought. I didn't know how to stand on my feet, how to give, how to listen.

Laura and Romeo held hands looking at the ground and mumbling to each other. Maria walked away, laughing with Claudia, Blondie in tow. Even Veronica the Airhead was joking, her friends patting her back full of pride for her performance. One of them said to her, "At least you made it *on* the team!"

I had not replaced my old buddies, yet. I was in decent terms with everyone, but I wasn't special or indispensable to anyone. Hopefully, one day someone would find me and make me happy. Jesus wasn't, so far.

I laughed at my silliness and pedaled home, seeing Nico in the distance on his own bike, flying solo: so strong, careless, untouchable.

The sweet and intense smell of our neighbor's jasmine hedge pulled me from my stray thoughts back to summer, filling my heart with the familiar crave for freedom, and dissipating the last remnants of melancholy.

The afternoon of the last day of school was the most exciting time of the year; I had the whole summer ahead of me, three months of sun, sea, books, and oversleeping. I was ready to leave school drama far behind.

June days were hot, but still clear and lush. Everything was renewed and mysterious beneath a layer of dew, excitement and stars.

Standing with Sonia in my backyard, looking at the small new beech tree that Starry had just planted, I asked, "Sonia, do you realize that for three full months we are free with no obligations whatsoever?"

The blinding sunlight rendered the colors so bright to be intoxicating. A fly buzzed, tearing through the sweltering heat.

Sonia rolled her eyes, looking bored. "Gee Lee, did you just figure that out?"

"Of course not, I'm just saying that it's all ahead of us!"

"Yeah, right. Homework and boredom. I can't wait to go to Ostia and see Ermanno."

"Well, as soon as the swimming pool opens, it will be a blast."

"Which reminds me, what are you gonna do about your legs?"

"What do you mean?"

"Well, don't you have *hair* on your legs?"

"No." My lack of hormones was at least good for something.

"*Really*?" She looked at me and said, "And what's *that*?"

"That *blond fuzz*? You can't even see it!"

"Oh, I see it all right," Sonia answered. "My legs are just the same."

"And why is that *bad*? Who cares?"

"Well, boys care! Your legs have to be smooth and hairless! Didn't you see the razor ads on TV?"

"I guess." She stared at me. I added, "Wait for me here."

I snuck upstairs, eyed Starry's purse on Grandpa's old rocking chair, and reached for her wallet, scrambling to get five-thousand liras out: just enough to buy plastic razors. I threw the wallet back and ran out, guilty as hell.

It never occurred to me to ask for money for plastic razors. Starry was so uptight with cash. There was never enough, and I was too freaking ashamed to tell her what I needed it for. I figured she wouldn't notice. Hopefully Jesus wouldn't either.

"Dear Jesus, please make this summer the best ever, and please get rid of leg hair, it's a minor fix, and make me and everyone else happy with good reason. Amen."

One of my wishes would be granted.

On June 15, pool-opening day, I was beside myself with excitement. It took all of it to coerce Sonia into a swimsuit and drag her there.

Glad to impress her with my connections, I waved at the giant, hairy lifeguard, "Hi Roberto!"

He grunted. Sonia did *not* look impressed. I showed him my season pass and Sonia paid the three-thousand liras for the day. We laid our towels on the grass and I shed my clothes, ready to jump into the water in my athletic one-piece.

Sonia shot up an eyebrow. "Are you crazy? The water is frigid."

"It's not so bad," I lied. "We'll warm up playing volleyball or something. Come on!"

"I don't think so. I'd rather lie in the sun."

"Okay," I gave up, pulling out *The Cosmicomics* by Calvino.

Three boys around fifteen walked in, making a

ruckus, pushing each other and laughing. Sonia's antennas perked up. She pulled out her *Cioè* magazine as a cover while darting furtive glances from behind her red-rimmed sunglasses at the three guys. They plopped on the grass on the opposite side of the pool to play cards.

"Oh my, and who's *that*?" Sonia purred, in her yellow bikini.

"No idea. Who cares?" I replied, worried. The three looked dangerous: much older than us, and rowdy.

"The middle one is really hot," she said.

Oh, boy.

A fourth kid came in, welcomed by the others with loud jesting and shoulder punches. The four put their swimming caps on and danced around the shower, pushing each other. They threw in the latecomer and then followed. They dove from the trampoline and played ball. Both Sonia and I looked at them longingly, for very different reasons.

I so wish I was a guy.

"Wanna go for a swim?" Sonia asked, eyes glued to her hunk of choice.

"Yes!"

We managed our own shower dance, Sonia screeching and squirming, me trying to become invisible. We got into the water.

"Wanna play ball?" I asked.

She shook her head, leaning back on the edge of

the pool, flashing big smiles towards the guys.

Truth hit me like a punch from Terence Hill, my favorite spaghetti western actor. I had gone from the leader of the Lone Wolf Gang, a bunch of kids my age with whom I used to spend summers, to being Sonia's wingwoman.

Sonia smiled again, taking off her swimming cap and shaking her wet curls in the sun, batting her eyelashes. Worse, were the darn kids going to drown me and steal my best if not only friend?

Meanwhile, their gang had grown with newcomers. One of them said, loud enough for us to hear, "Man, she's staring at you, I'm telling ya!"

I put my head underwater trying to cool off my face. Furious, I reemerged. "See? I told you!"

But Sonia giggled, ogling the clueless dude and answering, "I sure was!"

I saw what happened next as if in slo-mo. The kids looked at each other grinning and then waded toward us.

Oh, merda.

I jumped out of the pool. "Sonia let's go."

She gritted her teeth to keep her smile bright and say, "Don't you. Freaking. Move."

"Oh, *yeah*?" I walked away, furious, letting her simmer in her shame by herself.

She chatted with the kids for a while, fortunately exchanging pleasantries from what I gathered while hiding behind my book.

When they left the water, Sonia stomped toward me. "What's wrong with you, Lee?"

"What's wrong with *me*? What's wrong with *you*!"

Sonia made a show of drying herself with the towel. "I just made some new friends. They're nice, not to mention Valerio, the super hot one. Let's move our towels close to theirs, come on!"

She didn't leave me the time to retort, dragging her stuff around the pool. I hated being bossed, and I didn't want to be her shadow, but I couldn't leave her by herself either.

I huffed, grabbed my stuff and followed her. When I reached the small group, I dropped my things at the edge of the gathering and sat. Sonia had squeezed herself right in the middle where she enjoyed the spotlight.

A guy said, "Check that out! Isn't that *little Leda*?"

I winced and peeked amidst the crowd to discover Francesco's older brother. Francesco had been a member of the Lone Wolf Gang. It was weird to hang out with his brother, Oli, the one who had taught him his legendary cannonball dives.

"Oh, hi," I said blushing and hoping he had not heard about our juvenile gang. Good thing Francesco wasn't around to share our secret. Or was he?

"Lee!" Francesco yelled joining the group from the pool's entrance. "I see you made it in the older crop." He was chubby, with short black hair and a mischievous grin.

"I guess, *kid*." Francesco was two years younger than me.

"Well, welcome to *the Company*, Lee! That's how we call ourselves!" He gestured at the surrounding kids, beaming, full of pride.

Oli mussed the hair of his little brother, chuckling, then he added, "Well, Lee, you sure grew up!"

I blurted, "Yeah, you too," causing an uproar of laughter.

I dropped my gaze to my feet. With my peers I played the tough-tomboy card, but here I had no past and I sure did not look intimidating. This allowed me a chance to present myself differently, more like… a girl? Sonia leaned on Valerio. I couldn't nor would want to do any of the things *she* was doing. *Ever*.

Meanwhile, Valerio teased, "Yes, Oli, you've grown but only around the waist!"

Oli was on the rotund side, like his little brother, but he didn't seem to care and his loud laughter covered that of everyone else. At least no one laughed *at me*, in particular.

The chance to walk out of my tomboy persona was inebriating and terrifying at the same time. I didn't like Lee anymore, but I had no idea about what the next version entailed. Old Lee could pretend she didn't care and walk away. Instead, if I found and shared even just one piece of the puzzle that was the real me and people laughed at it, what would I do? I couldn't change who I was, only the person I pretended to be. If anyone told me that the real me was wrong, very much like I suspected, I would die of shame, humiliation, and loneliness.

"And what are *you* thinking about, so intently?" someone asked me.

I was not invisible after all. I turned to the newcomer: the most amazing guy I had ever dreamed of. My jaw dropped. He let his backpack fall on the grass and sat beside me. His big sunglasses, tuned in my direction, hid his eyes. Brown hair fell over his forehead. He looked older and as hot as hell. Could I forget Nico for a day?

11

Baciare, to Kiss

I stared at the gorgeous newcomer, trying hard to swallow. I couldn't. My tongue must have gotten stuck mid-way.

I coughed, then uttered, "Ah, me? I… nothing." I moved aside to increase the distance between us.

He leaned closer and pulled down his sunglasses revealing the most intense, deep brown eyes I had ever seen. "*Really*? You seemed lost in space."

"Story of my life." I smirked, impressed by his perceptiveness.

He smiled, and I almost died. "Giovanni." He offered me his hand, and I shook it.

"Leda. Ah, how old are you?" I dared, melting under his gaze, and wishing I had the guts to steal his sunglasses to hide my eyes at least.

"Sixteen, you?"

The world crashed on me. I smiled like an idiot as I stood up and rushed away hoping he'd forget we had spoken. I had finally met an awesome guy who did not look like a thug and he was *four years* older than me?

"Leda! Did I say something wrong?" Giovanni caught up with me.

Really? No one ever had run after me. *Oh, man.* "Ah, no… I'm sorry… I, um, realized… I didn't… Never mind!" I tried to smile but felt as if someone had dropped a sixteen-ton anvil on my pinkie.

Yet, he smiled back. Now he was standing, and I admired his sculpted *Baywatch* body. Okay, I had hormones, after all. I felt stupid, brainless, and exposed.

"Is everything *really* okay?" He tilted his head sideways waking me up from my ogling session.

"*Merda*! Yes. No. I mean, *What*?" I hid my face in *my* hands.

"You're something else," he said, startled. He continued, "So, how old are *you*?"

I considered lying, but why? Not like I stood a chance. "Twelve," I admitted. "*Almost* twelve. You could be my father." I added, trying to joke and betraying my less-than-holy thoughts.

He stared at me, horrified. "Your *father*? Geez, I might have been precocious, but not *that* precocious!"

Did he say *precocious*? My eyes filled to the brim with stars. Nothing gave me the hots like a fancy word.

He laughed. "At most, I could be your big brother."

Disappointment washed over me. "Yo, Dad, sure. Come on, let's go back with everyone else."

I walked away, hoping he didn't guess my childish delusion. I wanted to look him in the eye, flaunting the same self-assurance that Sonia showered on Valerio and anyone else around her, but there was no way.

The kids in the Company ranged in age between ten to seventeen since they could not get a driving license till eighteen and that the suburban gated communities were far from each other. Local kids stuck together, older siblings with their younger ones in tow.

The afternoon flew by in a blur of swimming, playing ball, and diving. I held back from most games, knowing I would have gone into ninja-mode and freaked out everyone. Girls had better not win, in fact they had better not play at all; it was in*appropriate*. With some luck, the Company would mistake my hesitation for shyness.

"Wanna come over to watch the game on Tuesday?" Oli asked Valerio over a match of *Scopa*, the complicated yet popular card game.

"Sure thing, man! Is that cool with your

Grumpy? I mean, with your Grandpa?" He chuckled.

Oli laughed. "Yeah, I'm sure he'll quit porn to watch it, too. Are you all in?"

The crowd answered with enthusiasm offering to bring chips, beers, and other snacks.

"What game?" Sonia asked.

Really? The entire country had been in an uproar about the 14th FIFA world cup. Every four years Italy went into a frenzy for the soccer world cup, but this year the games were taking place in our own beloved country and fanaticism had reached a whole new level. We had won the first two games in our group. Italians playing in Italy were hard to beat. Soccer was the national sport, and we were as boisterous as they come.

Ten bewildered faces turned toward Sonia. Martino, Valerio's ten-year-old brother, answered, "Italy, um, the World Cup?"

"Ah! I'm in!" Sonia laughed, clearing the awkward moment and overlooking that no one had invited her.

She had ignored me most of the afternoon, leaving me torn between pangs of jealousy and the excitement of gawking at Giovanni.

As the afternoon turned golden Oli proposed, "But for now, how about a couple of rounds of *dire, fare, baciare*?"

Dire, fare, baciare, —to say, to dare, to kiss— was

the Italian spin on truth or dare.

I looked at Giovanni who was winking at Oli, and my stomach imploded.

The only rule of the game was: boys asked girls, girls asked boys, which sucked because Sonia and I were the only girls. It could have been only her. I hated her phony behavior at the same time wanting nothing more than being able to pull it off myself. Giovanni was also on the margin of the action, by choice, reading a book.

I tried not to hyperventilate.

Oli asked, "Whose birthday was more recent?"

"Mine was two weeks ago," the kid who had been thrown into the pool earlier answered, his gaze not leaving Sonia. He seemed a couple of years older than me, with wild golden hair and hazel eyes. He looked like the surfers on the American shows.

"All right, Alex, then you start."

Alex shrugged. "If you insist. Sonia!"

Sonia feigned surprise. "Who, me? No way!" She squirmed.

"Oh, yeah, you. So, to say, to do, to kiss, letter, or testament?"

Sonia put a finger to her chin, lifting her big green eyes to the sky.

I suggested. "Choose to say!"

"No way!" she replied. "Ah, letter."

Everyone gathered around them as Sonia bent

forward to let Alex write on her back with his finger. She had to guess what he was writing, and he made it as painful as possible, slapping her butt hard to add the stamp. Letter and testament *had to* be unpleasant to make the other choices more alluring.

"And… SENT!" Alex kicked Sonia in the butt to mail her in an uproar of laughter from the crowd.

Sonia turned, massaging her behind. "I'll get you back, Alex, just you wait!"

He winked. "You could, right now."

"No, no." Sonia looked around, choosing her victim. "I pick… Valerio!"

Of course.

I glimpsed Giovanni smirking and rolling his eyes. Valerio's darker skin softened the harsh lines of his angular face. It was comical to watch him dealing with —or rather trying not to deal with— Sonia.

He looked sideways, his mouth pressed in a line, and then uttered, "To say."

"Okay." Sonia asked, "Do you like anyone?"

"I sure do," Valerio answered, mischief in his eyes at how easy he had gotten away.

"Who?"

"One question, one answer. Now it's *my* turn."

Sonia whined, "Hey, but that's not fair!"

Everyone giggled and Oli said, "You should choose your questions better, Sonia. Obviously you're a rookie playing against pros. Ain't that right, Gio?"

Giovanni looked up from his book and cracked his knuckles. Everyone laughed.

Valerio smirked. "Speaking of professionals, my turn to torture. Sonia!"

She looked at him as he were a jar of Nutella and said, without wasting time to complain, "To kiss."

"Oooooooh!" The crowd, including me, exploded in surprise. Nobody *ever* chose to kiss.

Sonia blushed while explaining, "Yeah, well, no more pain for me and I'm not gonna give my secrets away, so…"

"As you wish." Valerio snatched a black t-shirt from the grass to blindfold Sonia. The guys stood in front of her, elbowing each other and pointing at her. Gio was elbowing like everyone else, laughing with Oli.

She was supposed to grope. The first finger she touched would be her *victim*, but she seized Valerio's hand without hesitation. Clearly she could see through the t-shirt, but it didn't matter much since both Giovanni and Oli had stepped back at the last moment throwing Valerio, recalcitrant, toward her.

Valerio protested, "What the eff, man! Chill!"

But it was useless. The moment Sonia seized Valerio's finger everyone chanted, "KISS! KISS!

KISS! KISS!"

Sonia removed the blindfold, squealing and pretending to blush. The crowd quieted among giggles and elbows to the sides. Sonia looked up at Valerio, his eyes as stern as ever, her big green ones peeking through her long lashes. The late afternoon's sun made Sonia's strawberry blond curls shine like copper. Even with her child's face, she was striking in the sweet summer breeze.

The only one not snickering was Alex, who tried to look bored but was throwing daggers at Valerio, who played it tough and was credible, too. Valerio's aloofness agreed with his deep-set, black eyes and cropped black hair. He was tall and lean, masculine, and had a perennial frown. He scared me.

Sonia and Valerio stood in front of each other thirty centimeters apart: he looked serious and irritated, she squirmed and blushed.

I had never kissed anyone and wondered how many of the surrounding kids had. Not too many, judging by the dead silence surrounding the scene.

Sonia said, "But… here? In front of everyone?"

Francesco, Oli's little brother, exclaimed, "Geez, girl, what do you want to do with this guy, babies?" Everyone laughed and Sonia stuck her tongue out.

As silence fell back, I watched Sonia's silhouette approaching Valerio's in the sunset. In front of everyone, she brought her face close to his, which became more and more astounded as she gave him a peck on the lips.

The whole thing would have been more romantic if Oli hadn't grabbed Valerio's *culo* right when Sonia kissed him. She had barely planted her lips on Valerio that he turned toward Oli, outraged, to chased him around the pool. They both ended up into the water and, within seconds, everyone followed.

The pool closed at 8 PM, dinnertime.

While everyone gathered their belongings, Alex asked, "So, Sonia, are you guys coming out tonight?"

You guys meant Sonia. I didn't care. Starry wouldn't let me out, and Sonia's parents were even stricter. At least I wouldn't have to play the wingwoman role any further.

"Yes, of course!" Sonia replied. "At what time? Where?"

"We meet at the tennis courts around nine, nine-thirty. See you then!" Oli answered, passing us by with Gio.

Sonia looked at me, radiant. "Lee, come to my house first, okay?"

She hadn't even freaking *asked* me. At a loss, I used Nico's strategy: I feigned disinterest. I shrugged and kept walking. Sonia remained puzzled as if my acting against her wishes reminded her I was a real person capable of independent thoughts. Her face darkened, but it was nothing compared to Alex's.

He said, "Lee, we're just gonna be around the Pro and I'm sure your parents know mine… and everyone else's."

He was right, all grown-ups knew each other, at least by name, in our little gated community.

Sonia dismissed my shrug. "He's right, Lee. Catch you later!"

I wanted to strangle her and decided right then I would never see the Company again.

After dinner, Starry lit up a cigarette while I loaded the dishwasher.

"So, how was the pool?" she asked.

"Fine."

"Who did you go with?"

"Sonia."

"Just the two of you?"

"Yeah. We met some kids there."

"*Kids*? Which kids?"

"Um… the Marzellis, Farantis, Bonomos…"

"Oh, my! And how are *they*?"

"Fine. *Why*?"

Mom smiled. "I remember most of their parents from when we bought the house, and I'm curious about how their kids turned up. Anyone you liked?"

I blushed, but the doorbell saved my life. Starry and I looked at each other, puzzled and I stood up to answer. Sonia's silhouette at the gate told me I was in trouble. She never called. It was typically me showing up at her house. Sure enough, she had her drama stance on: long legs apart, hands on her hips. I couldn't tell her expression but I guessed she had a frown.

She blurted, "So, what's your problem?"

I opened my mouth to retort, but Alex's voice, a lot kinder, said, "Are you coming out?"

He was behind Sonia, in the dark, which was why I had not seen him. It was sweet that they had bothered to come to my place to check on me, even with the attitude, but I didn't want to go out to feel ignored and inadequate.

"No, I'll stick here tonight."

Not to mention Giovanni. I recalled his smile, his ability to be above the rowdiness, yet part of it. Everyone respected him. He was reading a book, for goodness' sake, and had even said *precocious*.

Starry materialized behind me. "Come in, guys, come in!"

Ugh.

She buzzed the gate open and my friends walked

in, Sonia rolling her eyes, Alex with a swagger.

"Good evening, ma'am," Sonia said icily. Starry didn't like her, anyway.

Alex passed Sonia, took Starry's hand and kissed it, bowing. "Ma'am, it's an honor. I'm Alex Farno."

Starry chuckled, falling for the obvious flattery. He talked her ears off. Wow, Alex was a mom charmer. Sonia and I stared. At least my bestie forgot she was angry with me and glared at Alex instead, probably annoyed at not being the center of attention. He talked for a good ten minutes about his school, his parents, etcetera.

I had no idea where he was going till he concluded, "Well, it sure was a pleasure making your acquaintance, Miss Silvia. I'll bring your best to mother. Would you mind if Lee came out to play in the Pro tonight?"

"Of course not!" Starry turned to me. "Just be back by ten-thirty, okay? And don't do anything stupid!"

"But—"

Sonia interrupted me, "Let's go, already!"

And so I had no choice but to meet the Company, and hopefully Giovanni, again.

12

Hide and Seek

Sonia and Alex dragged me away into the maze of streets that was the Pro, dark in the summer night. The Pro with its homes, pool, and two tennis courts, was closed to external traffic and intruders. More than once a perfect stranger had rung our doorbell in desperation, asking for directions to get out.

We headed to the tennis courts parking lot where a decent-sized group had already gathered. Some sat on the short fencing wall, chatting and joking. Some smoked. Giovanni was nowhere in sight. The lot, which would have welcomed ten cars on its best day, was deserted.

I sighed. Sonia was wearing the shortest shorts ever with a tight top that showed her tummy and her still immature curves.

"Your mom let you out like *that*?" I whispered in her ear, or as close to it as I could get from my short vantage point.

She answered, "No, I snuck out and they'll be asleep when I get back!"

I snickered. She reminded me of a big Lolita with her red cheeks, green eyes, and golden locks. I hadn't even showered and was wearing dirty sneakers, jeans, and a ratty t-shirt.

Oh, well.

Oli exclaimed, "There *you* are, Lee! You made it!"

"Hey," I said.

God, had I been too harsh with the Company? It was not their fault if Sonia had put up such a show, even *I* had stared at her, and I was no teenage boy.

When everyone put out their cigarettes and settled on playing hide-and-seek, I got excited. *Awesome*! We would use the whole Pro as our playground.

It was a June summer night in all of its magic: fragrant with jasmine hedges and buzzing alive with evil mosquitos. Oli offered to be *it* first. As he turned us his back to count, we spread out looking for hiding spots. I knew Oli could outrun me, so I settled for a car that had a good view of the light pole he had chosen as a home base.

"… Eighteen, nineteen, twenty!" Oli spun at the

speed of light, pulling out three karate chops.

I almost giggled. I wondered how many eyes were staring at him from the darkness. Oli walked away, and I crept out of my hiding hole.

I was about to run when Oli screamed, "Alex!" He turned, running with Alex was in pursuit. Maybe Oli had seen me, but I took my chances, going after them. Their stomping and swearing at each other covered the noise of my steps.

Oli got to the light pole first, yelling, "Alex is down!"

I crept right behind him and touched the pole. "Free!"

Oli turned to face me, eyes big with disbelief. "And where the hell did you come from? My pocket?"

He emanated a charming confidence. Coming from his pocket didn't sound like a compliment. I forgot to act like a damsel in distress, feminine and helpless. A victory grin revealed what I truly was: a Teenage Mutant Ninja Turtle, the leader of the Lone Wolf Gang, and many other non-girly things.

Breathless from the run, I collapsed on the sidewalk. Alex joined me, his wild golden hair more disheveled than ever, smiling despite the fact that he was going to be *it* next. He sat by my side, and awkwardness crept back into me.

I wondered about Sonia. She was all talk and typically followed me and my plan. Not tonight.

Alex asked, "So, how old are you?"

"Twelve, almost," I confessed, ashamed to be so young. "You?"

"Fifteen."

God, he was *so* old! And Gio was even older. Funny how I kept thinking about him. I blushed.

Meanwhile, the Company reappeared, one at a time, like fireworks in the quiet of the night: a sudden galloping echoed by Oli's profuse swearing. Not too many freed themselves. Oli ran like a racehorse.

In the distance I heard the noise of a motorcycle. I loved bikes. When I was a kid, my crazy uncle Bedo had snuck me on his rallying rampages on the mountains around Grandma's summer house till we had been caught. I had been forbidden to look at a motorbike ever again.

The sound grew closer and distracted me from Alex, chatting. It was a gorgeous, red, racing bike. I would have given anything for a scooter on my fourteenth birthday, but that would not happen. My sister's unfortunate history with two-wheeled vehicles hadn't helped loosen our parents' grip on the topic. I frowned when the bike didn't follow the road but signaled left, pulling over into the tennis courts' parking lot, where we had gathered.

"Lee? Are you okay?" Alex asked, bemused.

I snapped my jaw shut. "Yes! I just… really like bikes," I explained, unable to peel my eyes off Gio, hopping off his sleek ride.

Really, Jesus? Really? Now he has a motorbike?

Just to break the silence, I asked, "And what music do you like?"

Alex ranted about Queen while I ogled Gio's face: the sweet brown eyes, the smile lighting up his square jaw, the messy hair. He turned to me and I snapped my head to the ground.

I'm such a dork.

"Hi!" He smiled to Alex and me.

"Hey," I answered turning toward Alex, hoping no one noticed the various shades of blushing I felt burning my cheeks.

Alex quirked an eyebrow. "Gio, do you need the speed devil to cover the two hundred meters between your house and the tennis courts?"

Gio laughed, and my heart gulped. He explained, "Well, it was a gift for my birthday, but my birthday's not till the end of July—"

"You turn sixteen?" I asked, hopeful to knock one year off the old man of my dreams.

"Ah, no. I turn seventeen."

Merda! *Really*? *COME ON*!

He sat at my side, talking to Alex, "Anyway, it's still in *burnishing* phase. I have to put five hundred kilometers on it before I can push it. So I'm driving it around the Pro to have it ready for my birthday."

"Yeah, whatever," Alex replied.

Behind us Oli yelled, "Valerio!"

I could see Gio's incredible smile even if I stared at my dirty, once cream-colored Converse chucks. He smelled *amazing*. Stuck between Alex and Gio, I was at risk of melting on the sidewalk. At least it would have helped me disappear, given that I had forgotten how to pretend that I didn't care about anything and that no one could hurt me.

Alex asked out loud, "How many missing? I don't see Sonia."

Valerio chimed in, "Martino is missing, too."

Alex yelled, "Two missing! Last one screams *free all*!"

Just then, Sonia emerged from a huge bush of forsythia, which was a yellow cloud of happiness in spring. Its bent, long branches covered with foliage provided excellent cover. It surprised me she had chosen such a dirty hiding place.

Oli spotted her right away. "Sonia!"

As he turned the other way, Martino shot from behind Sonia and almost made it to the light pole before Oli caught him mid-stride and swung him up high. "Tino! Caught ya!"

Martino laughed and protested at the same time. With Francesco, he was the only kid younger than me in the whole gang.

"All right!" Oli declared. "Shame on Alex. You're next!"

Alex huffed and stood up.

Sonia was gesturing for me to join her. Her face

was red, her eyes wide open, her mouth set on a grimace of panic, her arms flailing toward me. I knew she needed my immediate assistance. She looked like she had just sat on the end-of-the-world-button.

Nonetheless, sitting alone with Gio at my side prevented any movement on my part, voluntary or involuntary, at least judging by the fact that I was not breathing and my heart had stopped. His cologne was *a-maziiiiing*.

Sonia stormed toward me, a huge frown on her face. "What is *wrong* with you, Lee? I gotta talk to you! Come *on* already!"

She was my blessing and my curse. As much as I would have loved to sit by Gio for the rest of my short, non-breathing existence, I had plenty of time to make a fool out of myself.

"Leda, Leda, LEDA!" Sonia yelled while dragging me into a corner.

"Yeah," I mumbled back, still gaga.

Sonia spilled, "Something incredible happened!"

I answered, "I know…"

"*How*? Man, you *are* amazing!"

Of course, we were talking about the incredible things that happened to *her*, not my impossible love for seventeen-year-old Giovanni.

I stared into her bright eyes, full of surprise and expectation, and I did not feel like disappointing her, so, I guessed. "You and Valerio made out?"

What else would rev up Sonia so much?

"Oh my God, yes! How did you figure it out?"

"Well, I'm quite the Sherlock."

"*Who*?" she asked.

"Never mind." It didn't take a genius to come to my conclusions.

It was easy to impress my friend, but it made happy that she showered me again with affection; making out was good for her. I didn't let that distract me.

I asked, "So? What happened? Spill every detail!" I couldn't wait to get an insider point of view on the mysterious practice of sucking face.

"Well, while Oli counted, Valerio ran toward the tennis courts so I followed, but I lost him. I figured he hid beneath the big bush."

"Yeah, you came out from it."

"Right, at first I hesitated. Spiders terrify me, but Oli was through counting. I freaked out and almost ran, but a hand came out of the bush and dragged me under the branches."

"No way!"

"Yes way!" Sonia confirmed. "So I found myself in the dark, squatting close to him and *so freaking* excited!"

She squealed, stomping her feet on the ground for emphasis. I hung on her words, imagining myself stuck in the dark in a forsythia with Gio. Why did these things never happen to me?

"And?" I encouraged her.

"Well, we were so close, side by side, almost touching. Oli caught Alex, yelling, and startled me. My shoulder touched his, and so I leaned on him."

I so admired my shrewd friend!

Sonia continued, "After a couple of minutes he took my hand."

"Nooo!" I screamed.

"Shhhh! *Yes*! I was on the verge of a heart attack. We couldn't say anything because Oli could hear. I was so psyched. I realized it was now or never so I gave him a peck on the cheek."

"*Merda*!"

"Oh, that's *nothing*. My kiss awakened him or something. He turned and with no hesitation he brought his face close to mine and kissed me on the lips. Not like today at the pool, a full blown, all-out kiss!"

Had this really happened while I played the Teenage Mutant Ninja Turtle twenty meters away? Sonia knew what she wanted, and she made it happen.

I asked, "What do you mean an all-out kiss?"

She fidgeted, blushing more, if possible. "He was… well… really into it. I kind of lost myself into it, too. It was soft and amazing and then…" She covered her face with her hands jumping up and down, "And then he stuck his tongue out—"

"He *what*?"

"He kissed me with his tongue! Oh, my God, I feel like I'm gonna pass out." She plopped on the sidewalk as I stood facing her. She added, "Now I know what making out is all about."

"It sounds gross."

"But it wasn't. He's such an amazing kisser."

"So, are you together now?"

Her eyes went wide. "Well, that's not the whole story."

"What do you mean?"

Sonia looked dismal. "Well, we had just kissed. I was leaning on his shoulder catching my breath when Oli caught Valerio."

"Wait, *what*? I'm confused. Wasn't Valerio with you?"

"*Right*. I stared at the guy under the bush with me. He looked like Valerio. At first I thought Oli made a mistake, but then I Valerio cursed him, running for his life."

"Sonia, who did you make out with?" I asked, drowned between amusement and disbelief.

Sonia chewed on her lip. "Well, I freaked out and just got the hell out. I wasn't thinking about hide-and-seek anymore and Oli caught me right away. That's when Martino ran out from *our* hiding place."

"*What*? Martino? Little Martino? Ten-year-old Tino? Baby Martino?"

She covered her face with her hands. "Shhhh!

Stop it! Yes! Yes! The ten-year-old kid."

"*Cazzo*! Is it legal? You made out with a ten-year-old! And he was *good* at it, too?"

Adrenaline rumbled through my veins, what a fine mess. The two brothers looked alike, with their dark skin and mysterious demeanor.

Sonia nodded, between ecstatic and bewildered. "Oh, he was *fa*ntastic!"

I asked, "So what now? What did you say to him?"

"Nothing! I ran away and came to talk to you. What do I do, now?"

She looked at me, eyes full of hope, but this was too big, even for Sherlock. "Sonia, I have no idea. Tell him the truth and apologize."

"Yeah, right! And lose my face? Plus, what if he tells his brother? I've been so dumb!" Sonia was coming down from her making-out high and sounded more and more exasperated.

From my position, I didn't see Alex approaching, I only heard him say, "Hey you two, done with secrets? Ready for another round?"

I turned. Everyone was around Oli, ready to go again, including Gio. My Casio watch read 10:25 PM.

I stood up and said, "Sorry, man, time for me to go."

Sonia took the chance to disappear. "Yeah, I'm gonna walk her."

Alex shot daggers at me. I wondered what his face would have looked like if he had imagined what was happening in Sonialand.

He answered, “Fine. I’ll walk with you.”

Sonia grabbed my wrist and walked away while saying, “No, you won’t. I need Lee to myself.” Then she yelled to the whole Company, “‘Night everyone!”

“See you tomorrow at the pool!” Alex yelled back, dismayed.

Sonia sighed, ignoring him. “Here is what I'll do: nothing. I’ll pretend this mess never happened, and if he says something, I’ll deny every bit of it. Who’s gonna believe him, anyway?”

“True. Poor kid.”

“Poor kid? He got to make out with *me*! No, worse, he tricked me into it. It almost counts as assault! My first kiss, too!”

I pictured sweet, mellow Martino, and raised an eyebrow at my friend.

She looked at my face and ranted on, “Okay, maybe I’m a child molester, but that will be our little secret, yes?”

“Sure pedo, sweet dreams. Keep them at least PG13.”

She smacked me on the shoulder looking relieved and we hugged goodnight. Things were about to get complicated.

13

Bloody Love

Sonia might have found a solution to her awkward ordeal, but confusion overwhelmed me. I had gone through my night rites. I had petted Fuzzer the cat and locked him downstairs, closed my bedroom's window, stalked a few mosquitos and splattered them on the wall, fumigated the whole bedroom with bug spray (I hated the stuff on me), and I had sat on my bed under the mosquito net with my book open on my legs. My old blankie, Hairry, was by my side for comfort and support. Yet sleep did not come.

The familiarity of my room remained invisible beyond the halo of my nightstand light. My eyes stared into the blackness but looked inside, trying to recap the events of the evening and to recall the minimal verbal exchange with Gio.

The old, tough me must have been somewhere under the weird excitement and expectation, but I could not tell. All I could think about was Gio and his gorgeous smile. The dampness of the night lingering in my room heightened the fragrance of flowers, yet I held on to a trail of Gio's cologne. Nothing to do with Visoni's radioactive cloud; it was just a hint of scent I had smelled when he was close, too close. His smile haunted me at the other end of the subtle trail.

I'm such an idiot.

Despite the *Baron in the Trees*, spread open in my lap, my mind wandered weaving future scenarios, impossible conversations, remembering, and hoping.

It was the summer of 1990, the summer of the Italian FIFA world cup. I was almost twelve, and I was hopelessly in love.

"Dear Jesus, thank you, thank you so much. This is one amazing, powerful feeling you came up with, but please, please, please, could you focus it toward someone my age, who possibly likes me back? And please make me and everyone else happy with good reason and let me sleep well with no nightmares. Amen."

On Saturday morning I tossed and turned in my bed, trying to steal back into my dreams, disappearing into a fog of possibilities. I got up at 11:30 AM, time for my breakfast of cookies and Starry's questions about my new friends.

"Alex is such a nice guy, Leda! Such good manners. No wonder; his mom is such a stickler for the rules. She's Belgian, by the way, did you know? And he's soooo handsome!"

I didn't bite, telling her instead of our hide-and-seek game, leaving out Sonia's X-rated adventures, "… And then Gio came…" I sighed in spite of myself.

Starry stared. "You don't say. Do you like this Gio?"

It was impossible to hide anything from Starry. "Yeah."

Starry smiled intrigued. "And how old is he?"

I cringed. "Sixteen." I omitted the almost seventeen part.

Starry snapped, "Are you *out of your mind*?"

"Gee, calm down, Mom. He barely speaks to me."

"Ah, okay. I mean, I'm sorry, but it's better that way, right? He's too old, don't you think?"

"What I think doesn't matter much, Starry. It

ain't gonna happen."

"Good. I mean, right. But how come you like someone so much older?"

"I have no idea. His smile, his eyes. He reads, and he's funny. The others respect him, but he's not all rowdy and stuff. He's sweet, smells amazing and, wow, he has a motorbike, too!"

"He *what*?" I realized my naïve mistake too late. Starry had already launched on an anti-motorbike campaign. "Don't you dare get close to that thing Leda, you hear me?"

As if I had the option. I rolled my eyes regretting my honesty and went upstairs to put on my favorite swimsuit: one-piece, like all my swimsuits, but of soft, burgundy cotton. I layered on a tee and shorts, seized my bag and left.

Sonia was waiting for me at her house, bubbling with excitement at the idea of going to the pool. So much had changed in twenty-four hours!

She let me into her bedroom where she checked herself in the mirror. "How do I look in this bikini?" she asked.

"Great, Sonia. Let's go, already!"

"No, no, no, no, Lee. Let the boys wait for you. You *can't* show up first. If we're late, they'll wonder where we are and if we are going at all. Only then, we make our appearance as if we had nothing better to do."

"But *why*? I'd rather swim than watch you in front of a mirror."

"Because boys like a challenge, mystery. They like to be hunters and you're the prey. It's their instinct."

"I don't want to be *a prey* and good job with Valerio on that." I chuckled. "I'm sure he felt quite the hunter, and I'm not even talking about last night."

Sonia frowned, puckering lips at her image in the mirror. "Well, *fine*. I'll be more *subtle* today."

"And how do you know all these things?"

"I read, too!" She pointed at *Cioé*, the teen magazine on her bed.

No one expected me at the pool, and I was eager to see Giovanni, but I waited while Sonia selected an outfit, and decided it was late enough *to make an appearance*.

Like Sonia had planned, everyone was already in the sun. The colorful towels on the lawn looked like a big flower. Much to my surprise, Giovanni welcomed us from the lifeguard's chair, smiling behind his sunglasses. I almost fainted.

Sonia batted her lashes. "Hi, Gio! What are you

doing *there*?"

"Hi Lee, Sonia. Roberto, the lifeguard, is on vacation. I'll sub for him for two weeks."

On vacation?

I imagined Roberto in an office with suit and tie for two weeks, just to break the routine.

Sonia pressed, "But is it legal? You're not eighteen yet."

"Oh, he's old all right," I mumbled.

Gio turned his most amused, charming smile on me. "Isn't that right? I heard I could be *your father*."

"Yeah, Dad." I looked away, broken-hearted and trying to disappear.

He said, "Well, do me a favor, Lee. Put your bag on the ground for a second, will ya?"

I complied, puzzled. He stood. I tried not to stare at his abs and not to blush, failing at both.

He seized me and slung me over his shoulder to throw me in the pool. Fortunately, rather than sending him flat with a head-butt or maiming him with a bite, I screamed, panicked. I think the main cause of my strange behavior was that the last thing I wanted was to hurt this guy.

Gio smirked. "Your dad wouldn't do *this*. Would he?"

He threw me into the still deserted pool, clothes, shoes, and all.

I emerged just on time to see Alex throwing a screeching Sonia in right after me, and the rest of the crew followed. Gio had gone back to his lounge chair, smiling, poring over his book.

I jumped out. My shoes squelched as I walked to the towels, dripping, ignoring the mayhem in the water. I removed my soaking rags to lie in the sun.

I couldn't believe Gio had taken me in his arms.

Lying on the lawn I imagined a shark attacking me in the deep side of the pool, Gio diving in to save me. I paid no mind to the crew coming back to play cards. A girl sat beside me.

"Hi," she said. "Did you come to steal all my boys?"

I looked at her bright green eyes and found no hint of malice, just amusement. "I wish," I replied. "You're talking to the wrong girl." I nodded my head toward Sonia, who was playing cards, giggling.

"I know!" She burst out laughing. "Don't worry, I was hopeless even before she came." She winked.

She had such a genuine, charismatic way to herself, but she had a few extra pounds, as compared to the women that crowded our TV screens.

I smiled and offered my hand. "Leda."

"Klara," she replied with a hint of accent.

"Where are you from?" I asked.

"From Germany. My parents moved here three years ago."

"Wow, your Italian is flawless."

"Yet, you caught me." A bright smile lit up her pimply face.

Sonia's yelping caused us to turn. She whined, "You're *mean*!"

Cards were spread over the towels and hanging from Alex's hand for everyone to see. Francesco had dropped his. They stared at Valerio and Sonia. Alex's jaw clenched.

Valerio lay on his side, panicked, cards still in hand. "Oh, come on, already, stop it!" he yelled.

Sonia tried to beat him, or pretended to. She straddled him, trying to hit him or tickle him, making a lot of noise. For once, he did not seem to mind, and laughed at her half-hearted attempts. It was like watching a documentary on mating in the animal world.

Martino and Oli got out of the water, walking toward the towels. Oli smirked, but Martino was unreadable: not a smile, a flinch, or wrinkle disturbed his serene face, way too wise for his ten years. I remembered his kissing prowess and considered he had many secrets.

My eye caught a detail, and the blood froze in my veins. I jumped. "Sonia, come with me." She ignored me, squirming all over Valerio. "Sonia! COME ON!" I tried to communicate the urgency with my eyes and tone.

"One minute, geez!" She kept up her sensual skirmish, giggling.

I had no choice but to do what was right, even at the cost of looking like an insensitive, jealous *stronza*. She *was* my best friend after all.

"Sonia! NOW!" I seized her wrist like she had grabbed mine so many times, and half-dragged her away. Hate emanated from Sonia and her playmate. I hoped that at least Alex appreciated my effort.

I hauled Sonia to the bathroom.

"What's *your* problem?" she yelled, turning to face me. "Didn't you see me right on top of Valerio?"

"It was hard to miss," I answered, relaxing now that we were out of danger.

"So *what*? Are you *jealous*? Do you like him, too?" Her voice boomed in the empty restroom.

"Sonia, don't be a *cogliona*. Do you have *le tue cose* already?"

"My *what*?"

"Your period, menstruation. You know? *Le tue cose*, women's bleeding."

Your things, le tue cose in Italian, was how everyone referred to menstruation, which seemed to be too disgusting of a concept to enunciate, just like *penis* or *vagina*. Not like they were part of your body or something… Certain words were just not polite to say.

She frowned at me. "Ah, *that*. No. You? *Why*? For goodness' sake, couldn't you ask me *later*?"

I lost my patience. "No, Sonia, I *couldn't*! You're having your first one *right now*!"

Her eyes widened and her gaze dropped to her crotch. "What are you talking about?"

"Don't freak out, it's almost nothing. But from my, um, vantage point, I could see a little stain on your swimsuit. Go check, okay?" I hoped I hadn't imagined things because my bestie would kill me.

She rushed into a stall and said, "*Merda*! Right *now*?"

"I guess you jump-started your hormones last night." I tried to keep a straight face.

"My what?" Her voice came muffled through the door.

"Hormones, Sonia. Didn't you study the reproductive system?"

Sonia huffed. "*Cazzo*, Lee, what do I do?"

"Nothing. Let's go to your place. Your mom will have stuff."

She walked out of the bathroom stall, humbled, a hint of tears in her eyes. "I was… right on top of him. Oh, my God. Did he see it? Did anyone?"

We left and walked toward her house, across the street from the pool.

"Sonia, I doubt it. Males don't ponder about periods, even less when you're all hot and bothered, squirming on a half-naked dude."

She blushed. "I really was."

"You always are! Like my Grandma would say,

God punished you!" I laughed as she hit me and then pushed the gate to her place.

14

Hot and Bothered

Within an hour we walked back to the pool. Our disappearance had sparked much curiosity, and many questions and few answers welcomed our return. I liked to be part of the mystery. It would have been easy to solve: two girls running to the bathroom and returning with Sonia now refusing to get into the water, but boys didn't think that way. In their mind it was another ruse for Sonia to be at the center of attention, and they played along.

Sonia escaped the excitement by leading me to the swings at the end of the lawn, past the pool's metal fence. I sat on one and she took the other.

"So," Sonia started. "I'm confused."

"About?"

"Well, I liked Valerio, but he doesn't fall under

my spell."

I wondered if she had learned the cliché expression from one of her teen mags. "Weren't you making progress?" I asked.

"I don't get that vibe from him. Alex on the other hand is available, interested, and he's super hot but…"

I tried to recover from the shock of the adaptability of Sonia's crushes. "But what?"

"But I can't stop obsessing about Martino's kiss!"

"Oh, Jesus, Sonia, he's ten!"

"Almost eleven. Just one year younger than you."

"Seems like a lot." I imagined making out with Francesco, two years my junior, and almost gagged. Then I imagined Giovanni, five years my senior, and my knees melted.

Love is weird.

That night, back at the tennis courts to play hide-and-seek, Oli screamed, running toward the light pole, "Leda!"

He had caught me this time, but at least I wasn't first. Martino sat on the sidewalk, close to Gio, who must have arrived while I was hiding. I bit on a cuticle. It seemed natural to go chat with the two of them, given the otherwise empty parking lot. I focused on looking normal and sat beside the old man of my dreams.

Gio smiled, unaware of the effect that his smile had on my knees. "Caught, huh?"

"Yep." I would have loved to say so many things, engage him, make him laugh. Anything. Instead I stuck with my original *yep*.

Gio turned to chat with Martino, when I heard myself asking, "What's your cologne?"

Oh. My. God. Did I just ask that out loud?

I imagined the two of them laughing at my face holding their stomachs so they wouldn't explode. Instead Martino kept his usual stoic expression while Gio turned back as if I had dropped the most casual line of conversation.

"You like? It's *Fahrenheit*." He leaned closer to allow me to assess it better.

What do you do, not to look like a complete idiot in these situations? I moved away from him to keep my heart beating and looked into the night. "Yeah, it's nice…"

Still sitting on the sidewalk I hugged my knees to hide my burning face between my arms. I wanted to disappear, or at least become smaller, because the blush warming my cheeks might have glowed in the dark.

"Do you have fun with us?" Gio asked. "You seem different from Sonia."

"Ah. Yeah. You?"

His hands dangled between his legs. "Yeah. I'm

different from Sonia, too."

This was not going well. I wasn't sure if he was joking or if he thought me dumb. I did. So I said nothing, which did not boost my confidence either.

I snuck a peek at him; he was looking at Oli chasing Francesco. I sighed.

What am I doing?

A thin melancholy predicted my broken heart. Even with my brain half working I knew this was an impossible love like Terence Hill, Kevin Bacon, Charlie Sheen, and the guy from *the Princess Bride*: perfect and unattainable. Yet he was sitting *right there*.

He turned to me and I jumped. I thought he would speak, so I forced myself to hold his gaze and failed.

"Lee, are you coming to the pool tomorrow or not?" He repeated the question I had forgotten he had asked.

"Oh, yeah, sure. Sorry, I… I was thinking about something else." *Merda*. I sucked at this.

"You got a lot of sun today," he commented, concerned. "So, what were you thinking about?"

I jumped up, afraid my *sunburn* might worsen under his eyes. "Yo, Oli! Are you done yet?"

"Almost!" Oli yelled, dancing his way to the light pole. "Sonia! There you go. That's everyone."

Sonia stopped running, disappointed. Then she picked up bickering with Alex, all giggles. Martino ignored them.

"All right. I've gotta go. See you all tomorrow," I announced with my back still turned to Gio and Martino.

Gio stood up in all of his might, his button down open on a blue t-shirt. "Come on, I'll give you a ride," he said. His voice made my soul vibrate like the strings of a guitar.

Incredulous, I cursed my stupidity for taking a fancy to the elder of the group. I answered, "No thanks. No motorbikes for me. I'm not allowed within a meter of one."

I wanted nothing more in the world than to jump behind Gio on his bike, but I needed to stop my delusion, possibly without getting grounded for the whole summer.

"Really?" Gio smiled. "Your parents sound worse than mine. I'll take you home your way, then."

Not knowing how to handle the confusion and embarrassment that his kindness threw me in, I tried to clarify I was not the twelve-year-old that had the hots for the lifeguard. "Gee, it must be your paternal instinct," I said. He burst in laughter. "Goodnight, everyone!" I yelled to the general crowd gathered in small groups chatting and smoking.

Some answered, waved, or smiled. Sonia was still busy getting angry while Alex tickled her. I shrugged and walked toward home with Gio at my side pushing his bike.

"So, what do you do for fun?" he asked.

"You mean, besides being thrown in a pool with my clothes?"

He chuckled. "Yeah, beside that. It's good to know you enjoy it though. I can make sure it happens more often."

I pushed him away in jest, but recoiled, flinching at his warmth. His presence at my side took over the night. I felt safe, yet the real danger was inside of me. It was an obvious mistake to let this guy under my skin, but I had no choice. All I could do was pretend I didn't care, play it cool, and limit the damage by saving face.

"So, what *else* do you do for fun?" he asked.

"I read and play volleyball, too." I omitted tree climbing, cartoons, and video games.

Once at my gate, I got closer to him to say goodnight, but his sexy cologne became more intense and then the heat of his body beneath the shirt overwhelmed me. Never in my life had I noticed the scent or the warmth of anyone I hugged, and I hugged several people a day, yet I was sure they were not zombies.

What. The. Cazzo.

My brain was melting… and my body, too. This was new. I inhaled all the Fahrenheit I could. "Thanks, goodnight," I forced myself to say.

"Goodnight," Gio answered, his voice lower, in

my ear, since we were so close. I came back to my senses and pried myself off him running through the gate.

As soon as I got to my bedroom, I sat on the bed, rocking since I could not stay still. Hairry the blankie rested in my arms. I was wide-awake, as awake as I'd ever been, like after a nightmare but with no fear, only an incredible excitement, giddy with a sense of anticipation, of magic.

Every word we exchanged replayed in my mind, every smile, every step, the one hug. Like an idiot, I reran the same scene over and over in my head changing my lines and his, imagining what could have happened if I were older, smarter, prettier.

"Dear Jesus, thank you for Gio. Even if he doesn't like me that way, I like him a lot and I'll never be able to sleep again. It'll turn for the worse soon, but I don't think there's much I can do. You, on the contrary could… I'm not sure what…"

I kept losing track of my thoughts and my prayers never made it to the Amen. My mind always marooned on an image of Gio looking into my eyes, enraptured, as enraptured as I felt just remembering things that had never happened.

I threw myself on the bed, light still on, smothering my face into the pillow.

On the following day, once into the water, Oli organized a meditation session at the bottom of the pool. The game required no real mediation. It consisted of letting the air out of your lungs to sink the four meters separating the pool's bottom from the oxygen, then sit there cross-legged longer than anyone else.

I was the only girl playing and was very disappointed that any other male was better than me. I gave up my mediocre meditation sessions and observed my friends. Gio stared at the pool, doing his job.

Alex didn't play the game and grappled with Sonia instead. Klara tried to help her.

"Klara! Klara!" I called. She swam my way. I whispered, winking, "I think Sonia is okay."

She looked at the two: Sonia had jumped on Alex's back hugging his neck as he laughed running through the pool like a crazy horse. Klara brought a hand to her mouth to trap the secret she had just learned.

"I thought she had it for Valerio," she said.

"Beats me." I smiled to Klara. "What about you?"

"Giovanni, the one and only, the hottest in the world." She let out a long sigh.

She was one year older than me, but I still asked, "Isn't he too old?"

She recited, "You can't command your heart, you know? Plus, not like I stand a chance, but a girl can dream. How about you? Anyone?"

She had been so honest, I did not lie either. "You're preaching to the choir… I agree very much."

She laughed. "Join the fan club!" She swam out to the edge and got out to lie in the sun.

Martino sat on the grass, toweling his hair dry. He looked at Sonia and Alex. It was hard not to. It amazed me how an (almost) eleven-year-old boy could be so aloof. His big, black eyes, like open windows, took in everything happening around him, yet letting nothing out.

It would have been impossible to guess he had any connection to Sonia. Even knowing for a fact of their secret make-out session in the X-rated forsythia bush, his detachment made the whole story hard to believe. Yet, I was sure Sonia hadn't invented *that.*

I wished I had Martino's stone-face to keep my inappropriate feelings for Gio inaccessible to everyone but me, but it seemed as impossible as sitting at the bottom of the pool pretending I needed not to breathe. I felt like bursting.

Someone cannonballed close by distracting me from my thoughts. Gio emerged at my side.

"Coming out tonight?"

I stared straight ahead at stoic Martino. "Um, I guess so, why?"

"So I can give you a ride." He laughed.

"Not a good idea…" Before I knew it I was telling the lifeguard of my dreams the story of my crazy motorbike adventures with Uncle Bedo.

He laughed and listened and asked questions. While Gio's looks, demeanor, and cologne had been the base of my infatuation, his personality intrigued me even further and it didn't help with the whole giving up on him.

He wanted to become a lawyer to make sure evil jackasses did not take advantage of uneducated people. The lifeguards of *Baywatch* sucked by comparison.

He asked, "Are you coming over Friday night? We're all watching the *Zio Tibia Picture Show* at our house."

Hell, no.

Panic set in again. *Zio Tibia* (Uncle Tibia) was a terrifying puppet that introduced horror movies every Friday at 10:30 PM. I was so impressionable that in my younger years I had *seen* monsters at my bedside, spending whole nights reading, terrified of potential nightmares. Even Young Frankenstein has sent me packing to my bedroom.

"Ah, no. The show is too late for me," I answered.

I jumped out of the water interrupting our conversation, hurting with the regret and resentment due to a past full of monsters I had almost forgotten.

15

The Master Planner

That night the Company went to call my classmate, Laura the Gorgeous, back from the seaside. She was Martino and Valerio's neighbor and a long-standing member of the gang. As soon as her gaze met Valerio's, it was evident why he did not care for Sonia. She was staring at them, too.

Valerio's harsh features softened as he talked to Laura. "It was about time I saw you," he said.

He fixed a lock of blond hair behind her ear, and I smirked when even Laura, who had a lifetime of practice with boys, looked at her feet. Sonia threw daggers at her. She was not over Valerio after all.

Everyone greeted Laura, hugging her and exchanging a few words. I did, too. "It's so good to see you!" I said as we hugged.

"You too." She smiled.

I lowered my voice to a whisper, "I don't want to draw quick conclusions," I looked at Valerio off to the side, "but… and Romeo?" As far as I knew, Laura had been dating our hot classmate when the school had ended. Funny how that reminded me of Nico, in Sicily like every summer.

A light tan made Laura even prettier in her own dainty way. She had long blond hair and huge brown eyes. "Yeah, but Romeo was *ages* ago. You know, school is over and stuff."

"True." It had been *ages*, *weeks* even. I saw Gio approaching and tried to keep my cool.

"Hi, Lee."

"Hi, Gio." I was ecstatic he'd come straight to me. On the other hand I was right on the outskirts of the Company. Everybody else was chatting and smoking in small groups. Laura and Valerio whispered at each other beside me.

Alex yelled, in the background, "Two, two, two! My lips on you!"

He had seen a car plate with three same numbers in a row and crossed his fingers. Someone else had to uncross them for his wish to come true. Sonia refused. Alex ran after her, tickling her and pleading with his free hand. They made a hell of a noise.

Gio ignored them. He looked terrific in his usual jeans and button down shirt opened on a white t-shirt and he was still talking to me.

"I'm cleaning the basement for Friday night," he said. "It was the price to pay to party."

"Wow." I inhaled Fahrenheit, cursing its effect on my mushing brain. "I mean, that bad, huh?"

"Yeah, so will you come or not? It's at our house, my parents will be there. Can't your mom let you out later on a Friday night?"

Why does it matter?

My heart fluttered, hopeful and I answered, "I'll see what I can do, *Dad*."

Alex interrupted us, "Please Gio, please, uncross my fingers! I'm cramping!"

Sonia screamed from behind him, "Nooooo!"

Gio stared at Sonia and uncrossed Alex's fingers without flinching. He then pulled back with a hand the brown hair that fell on his forehead and winked at me ignoring Sonia's wails. Dizzy, I leaned on the short wall around Laura's backyard for support.

Laura's mom appeared on her doorstep. "Lauraaa! Come in, already! It's time!"

Laura the Gorgeous stood and yelled, "Coming!"

Valerio stood as well and leaned in to give her a peck on the cheek. There was more sensuality charged into that one simple gesture than in any ruse Sonia had conjured to get to Valerio's lips. I turned toward Sonia just in time to see her face shatter.

Laura's door closed and indistinct screeching and

jeering rose around Valerio.

"Hoot hoot!"

"Kissy boy!"

Sonia was livid.

Back to his usual, grumpy self, Valerio stated, "Don't be *stronzi*. We're just friends."

Sonia exploded in an instant smile and jumped to get a hold of his arm to rub all over him.

He shook her off saying, "Goodnight. I'm off." He walked through the gate next to Laura's.

Sonia was petrified. I nudged her side. "You okay?"

She was teary-eyed. "But *why*? Did I do something wrong?"

I shared my friend's sadness. "You have bad taste in men." I smiled.

She smiled, too, sniffling and swallowing her tears. "I'd never treat someone like that."

"Sonia, you're treating Alex much worse. At least, Valerio is not leading you."

I regretted my words as soon as Sonia's face frowned into storm mode. Alex was sitting on the sidewalk in a heap, looking at her.

Her features softened. "I thought I'd make Valerio jealous with Alex. I guess it didn't work, huh?"

"It would seem not."

Sonia huffed. "Okay, I get it. I'm hopeless. What about you and Gio, then? I mean, you're always glued to him, not like *you* have a chance."

The air left my lungs. If my unobservant bestie had figured it out, I was everyone's joke, for sure.

"What are you talking about?" I hissed. "He's too old! It's not like I'm trying... or anything."

"But you still like him, right?"

It was up to Sonia to show me that if I liked Gio there was no changing that. I looked down. "Just don't tell anyone, okay?"

The confession heartened me, so I illustrated the Uncle Tibia conundrum.

Sonia said, "What do you care about the movie? You don't have to watch. Just sit close to him, and maybe you can hug him pretending you're scared. Although in your case you won't have to pretend."

She winked, and I punched her arm. For once, Sonia had turned out to be the master planner.

The following day, I woke up with Sonia's voice. "Come on, Lee! Alex showed up at my door!"

I sat up on my bed, groggy, rubbing my eyes. "*What*?"

"He is waiting downstairs! Come on! I don't want to be alone with him!"

I yawned, stretching. "Geez, Sonia. Why not?" I grumbled. "He's much hotter than Valerio, anyway."

"You think so?" She chuckled. "Come on, move it!"

In no time we were roaming the streets of Arese. It was cloudy, and the pool was closed, so we opted to explore the abandoned Villa at the outskirts of town. I kept thinking about Gio, the goodnight hug that had melted my brain, and the *Zio Tibia* picture show, a few days ahead.

Sonia scampered up the seven feet brick wall surrounding the park of the villa using a kilometer marker on the state road as a step. Alex helped her up, groping. It brought back an unpleasant memory.

I hopped on the kilometer marker and growled, "Touch me and you're dead."

Alex stepped back and grinned, "Suit yourself. I can't wait to see how you get your pocket-sized-self up."

I jumped to the wall and pulled myself up with minimal effort, leaving Alex dumbfounded. He hadn't suspected that Sonia's insignificant pawn was a Teenage Mutant Ninja Turtle.

The three of us dropped on the other side. We were in a lush forest. The house was barely visible in the distance like in *The Secret Garden* by Burnett: so close to the rest of town, yet so big and secluded.

A mischievous plan hatched in my head. I proposed, "Hide and seek, anyone?"

Sonia ended up being *it* first. She closed her eyes sitting on a carved marble bench covered in moss on the top of a small hill and counted. I followed Alex and pulled his shirt.

"What?"

"Alex, you like Sonia, don't you?"

He turned beet-red. "Is it that obvious?"

We hid into a bush. "Well, let's say I noticed, but you'll never get her by drooling. Go hide with her and kiss her. Be bold!"

"Are you *insane*? I'll just ask her if she wants to be my girlfriend."

I slapped my forehead. "Since you're at it, you might as well ask her dad's permission first."

"*Should I*?"

"Geez, Alex! You're all talk, aren't you? I was joking."

"Oh, thank God."

There was more to this kid than I had assumed. Gallantry and mischief played in his hazel eyes, glinting with the sun finally filtering through the leaves. Mm… What if the pool had opened? My thoughts strayed to Gio again. I had it bad.

I shot out of our hiding hole to get caught and give Alex a chance. It took effort to get Sonia to catch me.

Alex popped out from the other side of the hill and ran for the bench which was the home base. "Free!"

I smiled. "What was that Alex?"

"Free?" He frowned.

"You hear, Sonia? He's *free*."

Sonia kicked me in the butt, and we reached Alex at the marble bench. He dropped his gaze to the dirt path, blushing. I wished someone looked at me with those same bubbly, gushy feelings that were making Alex so flustered and my whole being vibrate just at the idea of Gio sprawled in his freaking lifeguard chair.

Alex mussed the hair on the back of his head. "Wanna play truth or dare instead?" He looked away.

Good move!

A coy smile spread over Sonia's face. "Why not?"

Alex asked, "Sonia! Have you ever made out with anyone?"

Sonia went from healthy glow to hospitalization-grade sunburn in the blink of an eye. Her unforgettable session with Martino was no conversation piece.

She replied, "But I didn't choose truth or dare, yet! I choose dare!"

Alex sputtered, "*Really*?" Sonia nodded, biting her lip. Alex looked away and said, "Kiss me."

Bravo, Alex!

Sonia's elation and embarrassment radiated from her every pore, but she had to pretend she was horrified. "No waaaay!" She giggled, "I hate you!"

Gag.

As she played out her act, Alex looked at me and mouthed, "Thank you."

I winked and said, "Geez Sonia, let's get on with this already! Rules are rules. Give him the darn kiss!"

She faced Alex. His wild, dark blond hair was all over the place, the light making his eyes shine even in the shadow of the trees. His lips parted with surprise. He looked at Sonia, who was his same height. She moved closer, and Alex closed his eyes. I couldn't stop staring. Sonia veered and gave him a peck on the cheek.

"*What?*" Alex blurted. "Sonia, on the lips!"

Barking came from the villa.

What the cazzo? Wasn't it abandoned?

Adrenaline washed over me as I glanced at my friends.

"RUN!" Alex yelled.

Panic echoed among us and within seconds we were running back toward the wall, two meters of brick, which looked like ten. We had no extraction plan. *Merda*!

"*Cazzo*! And now?" Sonia yelped, fidgeting and looking behind us as the barking came closer.

I clutched a tree branch and scampered up. Alex

followed me and we hoisted Sonia up, just as three dogs reached us, snapping.

I yelled, "Go, go, go, go!" We scuttled down the state road and ran till we couldn't anymore.

We stopped by the school, sweaty and short of breath.

Exhilarated as I hadn't been in a long time, I said, "So much for the *abandoned* villa."

Alex said, "Yeah, let's keep this a secret before someone gets in trouble."

Sonia nodded, still catching her breath, pocking at Alex's side as if she couldn't keep her hands off him.

They bickered the whole way back. I felt like an ornithologist during mating season, but more forlorn, wondering if I would spend the rest of my days as a diva's assistant or if someone, one day, would… fall for me, too.

Alex pulled out something of his pocket. "Oops! And what's this?"

He was holding a pair of my panties. Three for five-thousand liras at the Saturday market. Disbelief and shame flooded me.

"ARE YOU OUT OF YOUR MIND?" I screamed, snatching my undies back.

Sonia stuttered, "What? But… *how*?"

I stashed them in my bag screaming, "WHAT IS WRONG WITH YOU, DUDE? Who the hell are *you*? And where did you get *them*?"

Alex blushed, as if he had not expected my outburst, the *stronzo*. He raised his hands and rushed to say, “I found them, this morning, at your house, I swear. They were laying on the floor in the hallway and—”

“That’s the dirty laundry pile, you *coglione*!”

“I know.” He smirked.

Eeew!

I hit him on a shoulder as hard as I could.

“OW!”

“Don’t you dare complain! And you call yourself a *gentleman*? For your information, those are my sister’s. She’ll be furious,” I lied.

“Yeah, right.” He scoffed. “White cotton and straw hats? I doubt it.” He knew my sister was much older than me.

“Alex, we’re through!” I yelled, storming into the pool with the *stronzo* running after me.

“Lee, I’m so sorry! Lee?”

The Company was in the sun. Oli prodded, “And where do you three come from? What’s the big deal?”

“Nowhere!” Alex replied too fast as I said,

“Nothing!”

The most trivial secret causes an interest proportional to the time it stays hidden. I let Sonia enjoy the crowd and ambled to Gio’s chair. He was the only one who hadn’t uttered a word yet. I wanted to be as brave and shrewd as Sonia, and I wanted Gio to like me.

After a deep breath, I said, "Hi, Gio!"

Nothing. He didn't even look up, frowning at his book. I felt like an idiot. Was he just absorbed in his read? I stood there for a while before finding the courage to sit at the bottom of his chaise.

"Hey, what's up?" I asked.

Nothing.

Oh, God. Is it me? What did I do?

"Ah, is everything okay?" I asked again.

He growled, "Yes. *You*? Where the hell have you three been?" *His ga*ze followed mine to the swings, in the distance, where Sonia and Alex leaned toward each other, chatting.

Oh, my. Does he like Sonia, too? But she's only thirteen!

He put down his book and asked, friendlier, "So what's the verdict on Friday night?"

I smiled. "I'm a go. But only till 11:30."

"Cool. It will be fun." He stared past me at the swings.

Hope imploded within me, but Gio didn't care, did he? He was older and had helped me to blend in with the group, rather than being Lolita's shadow. *Merda*! I jumped up eyeing Sonia, who was walking back with Alex.

"Is everything okay?" Gio asked between amused and intrigued, I couldn't say. Nothing seemed okay at the moment.

"Yes," I lied, and I rushed away.

"I need to talk to you!" Sonia and I said, alarmed. We studied each other and laughed. Thank God for friends. She turned around, leading me back to the swings.

As soon as we sat she babbled, "Alex *asked* me!"

"Wow! So, you like him then!"

"Of course! He's so hot! What is there not to like?"

"Right." I smiled, proud of my successful plan. I wished I worked that way, too. "So, are you together? Did you kiss?"

She laughed. "Gee, Lee! Of course not! You *never* say yes right away. You look so easy if you do. Make them suffer, desire you. They have to believe they won't get you till the end."

"*They* do?" I asked and Sonia nodded. "Who's *they*?"

"Men, dummy."

"Ah." One would have been enough for me. "What did you say, then?"

"That I had to think about it. I'll say yes tomorrow, if I can hold back for that long." She threw a golden lock behind her head with a well-practiced move.

"Wow, brilliant! But now hear me out. You haven't told anyone I like Gio, right?"

"Uh…" I glared at her and she added, "Well… Alex. I mean, he asked and—"

"Sonia, what were you *thinking*? I'll be everyone's

laughingstock!"

Sonia rolled her eyes. "Lee, who friggin' cares? If he finds out, there's a chance in a million he might put the moves on you."

"I don't want him to, if he doesn't like me!"

Sonia was furious. "Geez, Lee! You think you're so special, don't you? Why would *he* ever like *you*? You're twelve, flat, and weird! The only reason I hung out with you at first was your big garden!" She jumped off the swing and stormed away.

Stronza.

I tromped back to the towels, gathered my clothes, the remainders of my heart, and I left.

16

Melting Point

That night I had no motivation to go out.

When the doorbell rang, I was watching *Chi l'ha Visto?* on TV with Starry.

She said, "See? It must be Sonia! She does care!"

I disguised my relief with an unlikely pout. At least, for the first time in history, my infuriating *bestie* had come to apologize.

I opened the door and froze, mystified. It was not Sonia at my door. A tall, still figure stood by a red motorbike.As the realization that Gio was standing at my gate dawned on me, I attempted to enunciate, "Yes?" My voice sounded choked and shrill.

A thousand thoughts crowded my head, which paradoxically seemed empty, just like when silence lasts so long it turns into a scream, and vice versa.

How is this possible?

What am I wearing?

Did Alex tell him?

Cazzo, cazzo, cazzo!

Sonia didn't come.

Sonia doesn't care.

Why is Gio at my house?

Gio's voice, low and unfaltering, interrupted my deafening silence "You didn't show up, so I came to get you. Are you coming out or what?"

"Ah, I don't know." I was surprised, confused, and embarrassed. "I was gonna stay in tonight."

Because I'm done running after you, making a fool of myself, and I'd rather keep my dignity, moping at home over my stronza best friend.

He insisted, "Oh, come on! It's already ten o'clock. Just for an hour?"

"Okay, wait a minute," I replied.

I crossed the foyer back to the living room, where Starry stood by the window, staring at the gatc. "Is that *Gio*?" Her words dripped ice.

"Ah, yes."

"I don't like this, *Leda*, not one bit. Why is *he* here?"

I was wondering the same thing. "Ah, he came to see if I'd go out."

Mom, the sweetest on the planet, could be the scariest on the planet, too.

"You listen up, Leda. I don't want you anywhere close to that motorcycle. And do nothing you wouldn't do if I were right there watching, understood?"

Creepy. "Yes, ma'am," I said, no irony in my voice. "Can I come back at eleven? It's ten already."

She studied me, then rummaged in her purse. "Here are the front door keys. I won't be up that late. This is a *big deal*, Leda. I am *trusting* you. If you screw up, you're grounded for the rest of summer. If you lose the keys, you're not getting them a second time. Understood?"

"Yes!" I tried hard not to beam at her, lest she took the offer back. I seize the keys, closed the door behind me, and met Gio still waiting at the gate.

He smiled. "Do you want a ride?" Damn him, he was so freaking hot.

I didn't even try to lie. "I would *love* a ride, but my mom is staring at us as we speak."

He flinched, throwing a glance toward the house. "Off we go, then!" He pushed his motorbike, and I walked at his side. When we rounded the bend, he turned to make me laugh. "Are we safe now?"

I did laugh. "Yes, yes. I hope so."

He jumped on the bike. "Come on!"

I cringed at the thought of betraying Mom's trust not five minutes after she had used it to threaten me, but I had no choice. I hopped on with no regrets, understanding what had gone through my sister's brain when she had eloped on a forbidden scooter.

With my arms wrapped around Gio, leaning against him, I was not sure where to put my hands. Anywhere seemed good and embarrassing at the same time. His familiar, much-coveted cologne inebriated me, and I spent the best five seconds of my life. We arrived at the tennis courts way too fast.

Thanks to my experience with Uncle Bedo's motorbike, I dismounted with ease, still in seventh-heaven, when Sonia assaulted me. "WHERE THE HELL WERE YOU?"

I recalled our argument, astounded by her tone. She was at fault yet dragged me to a corner of the empty parking lot by the tall hedge of one of the many houses of the Pro.

Gio laughed with Oli a few meters away. I answered, flatly, "I was at home. You mustn't have searched too hard."

Queen Lolita replied, "I waited for half an hour for you to come and call *me*."

I glared at her, arms crossed. "And why didn't *you* call *me*? Did my garden shrink?"

To my surprise Sonia looked down. "Sorry about that. It's not that way anymore."

My rage melted away. "It's all right."

She lit up like a Christmas tree. "So, what's up

with Gio? Why did he pick you up?" she asked with an incredulous smile that pushed hope into my battered heart. "*Miiiiii!*" she squeaked, short for *minchia*, which reminded me of Nico. She chuckled, nudging my side with her elbow.

I could have killed her. I didn't want to take a chance for Gio to hear us. "Stop it! Sonia, *come on*!"

"I said yes!" she blurted. "Since you were late…" She gave me a dirty look. "Alex came to call me and… well, I couldn't wait till tomorrow." She beamed. "But nobody knows! Say nothing!"

I wanted to ask why, but business first. "So, did you kiss?"

"No, maybe he's shy. I'll ask him to walk me home tonight."

The whole Company walked Laura back home, since it was ten-thirty, her curfew.

Alex and Sonia bickered. "Three, three, three, she loves me!" Alex said crossing his fingers, smirking at Sonia.

I asked Laura, walking at my side with Klara, "Where are Valerio and Tino?"

"They are visiting family friends for dinner."

Klara seized the opportunity. "So… You and Valerio?"

Laura smiled. "Well…"

"*Porca vacca*!" Klara said in her German accent, which was hysterical. Her tone did not express skepticism nor envy, only curiosity and happiness.

Laura said, "*Right*, but we grew up together and… it's weird."

I asked, "But you like him, right?"

"Yes, but he's so much older." I cringed. Valerio was fifteen, two years younger than Gio. Laura took a deep breath. "When we came home from the pool, he took my hand."

Awww, I was so jealous, but her tone implied that something was wrong.

Laura continued, "But then he… He scratched the tip of his finger against my palm, you know?" She blushed, and Klara and I looked at each other.

"Well," Laura explained. "My friend Goran, who's much older, actually he's my sister's friend, said it means—" she looked around with circumspection and concluded in a whisper, "that he wants to sleep with me!"

"*What*?" Klara and I blurted out.

"Shhhhhh!" Laura pleaded.

"But you're twelve!" I yelled-whispered.

"Not even!" she replied.

Klara chimed in, "Okay, what's the chance your friend was pulling your leg?"

Laura's eyes opened wide. "Ah, I didn't think of that."

"Or," I continued, "that Valerio has no clue and did it by chance?"

Laura smiled. "But how do I find out?"

"Let's ask Gio," Klara suggested. "He's older."

Nausea raised at the thought of what Gio might know or do with girls. "I will not give any detail away, yes?" Klara asked.

Laura nodded.

"Gioooooo!" Klara called.

Gio, behind us, chatting with Oli and Francesco, looked at us. Klara asked, "What does it mean when someone holds your hand and then scratches your palm with one finger?"

Gio and Oli looked at each other, puzzled. They shrugged, and Laura's shoulders slumped with relief. They noticed.

Oli teased, "Tell us, little Laura, what does it mean?"

"And above all," chimed in Gio. "Who might have been holding your hand?"

Klara snapped her head back, whispering, "I'm so sorry! I didn't say!"

Laura laughed. "It means someone is telling you a lie." She winked at us, giggling.

I admired her presence of mind. I stopped to tie my shoelace as Laura, still chatting with Klara, kept walking. Oli and the others caught up, pestering them with questions.

As I stood up to run after them, Gio's voice startled me. "So what does it *really* mean?" he asked.

I jumped, and he stepped closer so that my back touched his chest. I turned to stone as he leaned to whisper into my ear, "What does it mean, Leda? You can tell me."

I stepped away to increase the distance between us, tilting my head forward to cover my flushed face with my hair, which I had let loose to dry. It had gotten long, way past my shoulders.

"No-nothing," I stuttered. "That you're telling a lie," I repeated.

He walked beside me and took my hand, scratching the palm. He added, "I guess I called you on it, then."

Time stopped.

I would have liked to joke, to punch him, to scratch the palm of *his* hand, anything. Instead I stood there, his hand holding mine. Did he know what the gesture really meant? I thought not. He was still holding my hand. Had it been a minute? An hour? A second? Did I die? The more I tried to say something, the more I drowned in confusion and Fahrenheit. My embarrassment was liquid, red and hot. Was I melting?

Speechless, I put one foot in front of the other, but I could not feel the ground, only Gio's hand. The voices of our friends, closer to Laura's house reached me, unintelligible.

Is this happening?

My heart fluttered when Gio said, "Your hair is amazing. When did you cut it last?"

"Ah, a while." I swallowed. After Grandma had

painfully shown me how to *brush it,* I had opted for nobody to touch it ever again, including the hairdresser.

Meanwhile, everyone had made it to Laura's. What if someone turned and saw us?

I let go of his hand and said, "Come on, let's catch up."

I ran away, happy, scared, and confused, but most of all happy.

The following day was overcast. I didn't care because I was walking way above the clouds. Starry loaded her blue *Panda* car with her books and luggage for the night. When she left for Padua to take her finals, she was off after a few hugs, but this time she hesitated.

She let out a big sigh, and recited,

"With the helmet on his head
Not to hurt himself too bad,
He set off, spear at his side
Riding forth his equine ride."

"Hopefully it ends better, Starry."

The lines she quoted, introducing the comical adventures of *Valiant Anselmo* by Giovanni Visconti Venosta, ended up with the warrior dying of thirst drinking from a leaky helmet.

"Hopefully." Her gaze turned to stone. "You

behave. I'm gonna call you at 8 and 11 PM, and you'll better answer or there will be trouble."

"Yes, ma'am," I answered, and she drove off.

After Mom left, I called Sonia, who was not ready yet.

As she discarded one outfit after the other, I sat on her bed.

"Are you okay?" I asked.

She huffed and plopped beside me. The bed creaked.

She rubbed her face and said, "Alex is a *disaster*. Nothing happened."

"You mean, no amazing make out session under a forsythia bush?"

"No. I mean *no-thing*!. No making out at all, no kissing, not a peck on the cheek. He didn't hold my hand—" My breath caught and Sonia, noticing, said, "*Right*? He was all bold groping my *culo* when I was not available, and now…"

Wow, she was all business. "Does he need to adjust a little?" I suggested.

"Martino didn't."

"Oh, God. Sonia, you imprinted!"

"I *what*?" she asked, frowning. She hated it when I referenced obscure concepts.

I laughed. "My mom was studying this

psychologist, Lorenz or something, and he found out that—"

"Oh screw you and your books, Lee! This is serious. What do I do?"

I felt bad for pushing Sonia into Alex's arms. "Sonia, Tino set an impossible standard for anyone else to match, but he's *ten*."

She lowered her eyes. "Yeah, ten and mysterious. He never mentioned one word, not to me or anyone. He never spared me a smile or a glance afterward."

"And that's killing you, isn't it?"

"Yeah," she confessed. "I'll give Alex another chance, but if nothing happens…"

"Fair. Anyway, enough about you, hear me out. Gio took my hand!"

"Yeah, right!" She laughed. "And I'm pregnant."

"I sure hope not," I answered. I couldn't blame her skepticism since I hardly believed what had happened myself.

"*Seriously*?" she blurted. I nodded, and she added, "Like… was he kidding? Lost? Were *you* lost? WHAT THE *CAZZO*?"

"Well, he *was* kind of joking."

"A-Ha! I thought so…"

"Well, screw you, Sonia. It was amazing, and I got more action than you." I stuck my tongue out.

"That," she said, "might be true."

A few fat raindrops hit the window, which meant

the pool was closed, and I wouldn't see Gio all day.

"Well, that sucks," I declared.

Sonia suggested "Why don't we go to get our ears pierced?" I hesitated. "Come on!" Sonia said, grabbing her bag. "I've always wanted a second piercing!"

Her mom would kill her, but I followed her out. I was becoming girlier than ever. Starry would be elated when she came back, and hopefully Gio would be, too. Friday night and the Zio Tibia show were approaching at the speed of light. Sonia's master plan would deliver me straight into Gio's outrageously hot arms.

17

The Zio Tibia Picture Show

At dinner I devoured bread and Nutella and drank soda in front of *Bosco Adventure* cartoons.

At 8 PM sharp the phone rang. "*Pronto*?" I answered.

Pronto means ready in Italian, and it's the universal way to answer the phone since the times when an operator needed to connect you.

Starry's voice sounded cheerful through the receiver. "Hi, honey! It's me! Is everything okay?"

"Yup. Is the exam early tomorrow?"

"No, but I have to get up at dawn to write my name on the shee."

"What sheet?"

"The one that determines the order in which people take the exam."

"I see. Can't you write your name and go back to sleep?"

"Nope, or whoever comes next will rip the sheet off and start a new one."

"What a moronic method."

"Lee, you sound like your father."

"Isn't *moronic* a common word?"

"Not as common as one would think listening to him."

The conversation dwindled, so I began the ritual exchange of verbal exorcisms to warrant good luck during Mom's final. Italians are *that* superstitious.

"In the mouth of the wolf," I said.

Starry replied, "Death to the wolf."

"In the *culo* of the whale."

"Let's hope it doesn't shit."

"Between Fuzzer's paws."

"There's no way out," Starry replied. We had made up the last one ourselves.

"Goodnight, Mom."

"'Night, Lee."

I hung up, praying with all my might for her to pass her stats test.

That night Italy played Czechoslovakia for the 14th FIFA soccer world cup and the Company planned to watch the game at Oli and Francesco's. Self-conscious of my red, pierced ears, I let my hair loose, even if it was not wet from the pool.

I arrived at the seventh minute. Oli opened the door and ran back to the TV, yelling, "Come in, come in!"

"*Permesso?*"

It didn't matter he had told me to come in, any Italian walking into someone's house would ask for permission, *again.*

Kids packed the living room. Oli's infamous grumpy grandpa, whom I had known for years, slumped on a rocking chair puffing on his pipe.

I was pondering where to sit when the room exploded in an uproar. "GOAAAAAL!" everyone screamed, hugging each other and me, who happened to be in the way. Italy had scored.

Grumpy Grandpa smiled at me; it was a first. "And who's the lucky girl?" he asked, not recognizing me.

"That's Lee, Gramps." Oli said, eyes to the TV.

"You should marry her," Grandpa stated.

I had walked in and Italy had scored; that made me a keeper.

Oli said, "Francesco tried a while back. I heard it didn't go well."

"He did?" I asked, abashed, looking around for Oli's little brother, nowhere in sight. I recalled him challenging me as kids, following me around… It made more sense now.

Grandpa did not avert his eyes from the screen. "He didn't try hard enough. The girl didn't even notice. I can't believe you kids are my blood."

Everyone giggled, and I plopped on the floor, hiding my face behind my hair, leaning against Oli's couch.

Just then Francesco came out from the bathroom. "What did I miss?" he asked.

"A lot," Grandpa briefed him. "Oh, and Schillaci scored."

I looked at the TV trying hard to keep Martino's stoic face. After a few minutes I dared to assess the room. Sonia and Alex squeezed each other on a couch by Gio and Klara. Francesco and Oli shared the love seat behind me. Grandpa rocked on his chair, while Martino sat on the floor, like me.

At the seventy-eight minute Baggio sealed the deal: 2-0. The house exploded with cheer. Starry's 11 PM call approached. Not to bother anyone during the last ten minutes of the game, I snuck out while they were still celebrating. I gave a few high fives, screamed, and left, unseen.

Starry nailed the stats exam, so much for the Valiant Anselmo! I was angry from the unwarranted worry she had forced on me, but more pressing issues kept me busy. I had been planning my outfit for the Zio Tibia picture show for days by the time Friday came. I wore a brand new t-shirt with pink, blue, and green in it. I hated pink, but it made my eyes bright: blue and green at the same time.

Sonia's plan was to show up late, around ten, so that all the seats would be taken. Then we could squeeze in by our guy of choice.

At ten, Gio's mother opened the door for us. She looked gray, stern, and unhappy, which made sense with the recent teenage invasion in her basement.

"Hi," Sonia dismissed her walking by.

I offered my hand. "Good evening, ma'am. My name is Leda. It's nice to meet you."

She scowled letting my hand hanging.

Yikes.

I stepped inside, too. Sonia eyed the door to the basement, ajar. Festive noises came up the stairs. I absorbed as many details as I could about Gio's home: the objects he saw every day, where he grew up. A couple of pictures on a shelf called my attention, but Sonia clutched my wrist and dragged me down the stairs.

I protested, "Gee! What's biting you!"

"Oh, move it. I can't wait."

She was on a mission to make out with Alex: tonight or never. We emerged into the dark basement.

"Hi everyone!" Sonia greeted and a choir of voices answered.

I heard Alex's from the love seat in front of us. He was sharing it with Francesco.

"I want the presidential seat!" Sonia declared, walking there and collapsing in between them. I stalled. In the dim light around the big TV I couldn't tell people apart, but I didn't want to make it look like I was choosing either. So, when Francesco said, "Come on Lee, you can fit too," I sat where he made room: between himself and Sonia.

Great.

Sonia wrung around Alex as a vine, showing us her back. I turned to Francesco who made a funny face nodding at the two and then gave me two thumbs up.

I smiled back and relaxed. Everyone chatted, semi-following the end of whatever show was on. My eyes adjusted. Valerio stood up to pour himself soda by a table toward the back wall with several bottles on it. When he sat back, I saw Klara and Laura at his side.

Oli was on a third couch, Martino on the floor. Where the heck was Gio?

Steps trotted down the stairs and Gio's voice

announced, "Here we go! Freshly made!"

The smell of popcorn wafted through the basement. Klara patted the couch by her side, "Right here, Gio!"

He sat, munching and passing the bowl. I hated when popcorn got stuck in between my teeth, and now it had caused my plan to fail.

Uncle Tibia's puppet appeared on the screen, announcing *Fright Night Two.* The ugly doll (imagine Sesame Street gone wrong) made me jolt. It didn't take much.

There was no going back, and I couldn't believe I was stuck in front of a horror movie out of my own doing. I couldn't even look at Gio without turning my head.

Francesco scooted closer, and his body warmed mine. I hadn't been close to anyone in a long time, maybe since I was a young child, sleeping on my Mom. It was comforting since I felt less alone.

The movie began.

I ignored the fast succession of exsanguinations, vampire attacks, and transformations as much as I could. I closed my eyes, but that didn't help much.

Francesco put his arm on top of mine. Did he share my brotherly feelings or was he putting the moves on me? I flung my arm across my body at an awkward angle to avoid both him and Sonia's moving form as she sucked face with Alex. *Gross*! At least *her* plan had worked.

I turned the whole way just to glimpse Gio staring at the screen beside Klara. I had been such an idiot. Even Sonia had tried to warn me. Klara's words echoed in my head… *A girl can dream, right?* My house of cards fell into a pit full of vampires.

I closed my eyes again, trying to hold back a tear of humiliation, desolation, and outright terror. At least I was feeling something. At least stuff was happening to *me*. Out of the nest, I was exploring the world beyond my family, letting people figure me out since I hadn't. I would have rather drowned than stare at flip-flops by the pool like Baccellati.

I waited for curfew. Even without my crumbling expectations, this would go down as the worst evening of my life. At a quarter past eleven, after forty-five stoic minutes of blood sucking and ugly monsters, I jumped up at the commercial break. "All right everyone, goodnight!"

A few cries of protest lifted. "Come on! It's not halfway through!"

It was endearing, but a million liras would have not convinced me.

Gio's voice rose above the rest, "I can talk your mom into letting you stay a little longer…"

It was so easy to mistake his kindness for more in my enamored state, but I had learned my lesson.

"No, thank you." I smiled with effort. "Waking her up won't help." Gio stood up to walk me to the door. I protested, "Geez, Gio! Please, sit down, will ya?" I raised my hands to push him back on the couch, but I didn't dare to touch him. With a hint of melancholy I added, "Sit. Don't miss the movie for me. I can show myself out."

I walked upstairs because I didn't want to look at his face any longer, but he followed me. At his door I turned to say goodnight, but he closed it behind us.

I asked, "And where would *you* be going?"

"I'm walking you home. Or do you wanna walk by yourself with all those vampires lurking?" He was joking, but I was very much concerned about the lurking vampires.

I babbled, "But… and the movie?"

He opened the gate for me, "It was not that great, right?" He smiled.

I suppressed a stupid shiver down my back. We walked through the deserted Pro. Our steps echoed in the night. The sparse streetlights made our shadows dance in circles around us.

I tried to dismiss Gio's cologne, his hands gesturing in the night, his laughter as he chattered about the plot holes in the movie. His closeness overwhelmed me. How could I pretend that I was not in love with him? I hid the mayhem of feelings erupting in my chest behind a timid silence as Gio's presence claimed ownership of my thoughts and my heart.

When we reached my gate, the rustling of the

poplar leaves welcomed us. The sweet scent of jasmine saturated the night.

"A firefly!" I exclaimed pointing into the dark and jumping up and down. I had never seen fireflies in Arese.

Gio was silent. I turned, imagining him searching for the firefly, but his eyes were on me.

"Leda, listen, I really like you. Would you be my girlfriend?"

18

Fahrenheit and Vampires

I almost passed out.

It was like in those dreams where my body exploded in a car accident. I thought I was in one piece, but I was not sure I had woken up, yet. My head was empty. I realized that this was *it*, the climax of my life. Wasn't I whining just now that I had hit rock-bottom? Life had gotten me again.

Gio had chosen *me*. I closed my eyes to end the dream and wake up in my bed. When I reopened them I was still staring at our shoes. An inconceivable joy reverberated through me. Words failed me until a familiar echo took over me like an automatic pilot.

I mumbled, "I… I have to think about it." Bless Sonia and her life lessons!

Gio asked, "What do you mean? Do you like me or not?" He frowned, stepping away.

He was right. Sonia's reasoning, which had made so much sense a few days earlier, seemed nonsensical. I was an almost-twelve-year-old girl caught repeating things she did not understand. I mumbled, "I do… like you, but…"

He smiled, searching for my ground-aimed eyes. He was seventeen for God's sake.

Jesus, what do I do?

I remembered Starry's worry and Sonia's disbelief.

Is this a joke?

I concluded, hoping to disappear, "I… It's complicated."

Gio looked wounded. "You're not sure?"

Alarmed by his reaction I forced myself to admit, "No, I mean, yes… I like…. you… *a lot*…" turning beet-red.

How does anyone survive this?

The last thing I wanted to do was hurt him, but I wished I had bitten my tongue instead of confessing my feelings, because now I was vulnerable and at a disadvantage.

Gio did not laugh in my face. He listened with his head tilted, waiting to hear more, but this was way too much for me.

I lifted my gaze, trying to smile, but my expression was as frozen as Uncle Tibia's puppet's.

I said, "I'll see you tomorrow, okay?"

I spun around to run through the gate, but he seized my shoulder and pulled my back to his chest, which I had memorized during days of ogling at the pool.

Everything stopped.

The heat from him burned my skin through our thin summer clothes. I couldn't breathe. My brain melted between vampires, Fahrenheit, and Gio's arms. My hair stood on edge, and the hug lasted longer than normal between friends. It was a second and an eternity at the same time. When I stepped forward, he let me go.

"Goodnight!" I mumbled, and I ran through the gate in a mayhem of excitement, confusion, and disbelief, causing Fuzzer the cat to run for his life.

The familiar sound of the door closing behind me was comforting. The pallid light of the TV flickered in the living room, and I freaked out. Was I late? I tried to dispel the excessive turmoil from my face and peeked in to see my big sis Viola, rather than Starry.

"You're back!" I exclaimed. In my exhilarated state I hadn't noticed her car.

"Yup. College classes are over. How goes it, kiddo?" she replied.

"Ah, uh." *Freight Night Two* unfolded on the screen and I averted my eyes.

"Right-o. I sure hope this was *not* the movie Starry said you would watch with your new friends." Viola inspected me like doctor examining a patient.

"It was."

"You… look out of it." She sighed, turning the telly off.

"How did your exams go?" I asked, eager to change the topic.

Viola *smiled,* a sight as rare as beautiful. "*Awesome*. For the first time in my life I'm good at something, you know?" Before I had the chance to answer her smile waned and she added, "Eh, what would you know?"

Confused, I replied, "That's so cool! So, are you done for the summer?"

"Nu-uh, I have another final in July and one in September, but I figured I'd come here to study, so I can see Marta and get Starry to make me food."

"Wow, *that* desperate?"

"No shit." Campbell's soups and melted plastic only got her that far, apparently.

I smiled. "Well, goodnight. Good to see you!"

"Mm, Lee?" she called after me.

"Yeah?"

"The vampire stuff, it's all *stronzate*. Sleep well."

A mix of shame and happiness colored my heart.

"Thank you," I replied and she turned the TV back on.

"Dear Jesus, thanks for turning the most awful night of my life in the most memorable. I can't believe that…"

Again, my bedtime prayers kept derailing into sidetracks full of Fahrenheit and vampires. I took the best of half an hour to get to the *Amen* and I was not one wink closer to sleep.

I hugged Hairry. Giddy with unfamiliar feelings, I replayed the events of the evening. I read two lines from my book before staring into the darkness with a silly smile, remembering Gio's every word and gesture.

I muttered to myself, imitating his manly voice, "Leda, I like you very much."

I erupted in little screeching sounds and had to choke my face into the pillow. Love made me stupid, and I couldn't care less. Then I snapped my head around checking for vampires, and a shiver ran along my spine.

I sighed. Tic toc, tic toc, 1 AM.

Would you want to be my girlfriend? Or had he said *like*?

And the hug, my body leaning against his, that sweet, sweet embrace… If I smelled the shirt I wore earlier I could still imagine a note of Gio.

I sighed, rolling over. I seized my book, read a few pages. Tic toc, 3 AM. The quiet of the room contrasted with the chaos inside of me: feelings clashing like waves in a stormy sea.

I so wanted the night to be over to see Gio and not think of vampires. A noise startled me, and I stared at the edge of the halo of my nightstand light. Nothing. No vampires, no monsters, no Gio.

Tic toc, tic toc.

Even dawn, which in my most restless nights had brought me serenity and slumber, did nothing for me.

5 AM. I tiptoed to the hallway lit by an ashen light. A timid hue of yellow and then pink tinted the sky. The birds exploded in a sudden argument, scaring me. The street out of the window was deserted: no vampires in sight. Nor behind me, I gathered by turning to check the hallway. I went back to my bed and read till I heard Mom stirring. I waited long enough for her to drink her first morning coffee —she was unbearable before— and then I walked downstairs.

Starry almost choked on her espresso when she saw me at 8 AM on a Saturday, but she grunted a greeting. After her second round, each comprised of three espresso shots (no kidding) she looked at me bleary-eyed. "Everything okay?" The early hour made her smoker voice hoarser.

"Starry, Gio asked me," I blurted with no preamble.

"Asked you *what*?"

"Um, to be his girlfriend."

I was excited and terrified. Gio had concerned Starry, and I cared for her opinion.

"Let me finish my coffee first, will ya?"

Her expression suggested she would have gone back to bed rather than hearing my story, or back into the womb if that had been an option. I anticipated my news would have been better than espresso, but I was wrong. Disappointed, I waited for her to catch up.

She lit a cigarette. After a few minutes she asked, "So, what did this Gio guy do?" She inhaled.

I babbled out the whole story, leaving out only the vampires. With all my sleeping trouble she would have killed me I she found out I had watched a horror. Starry listened to every word and lit another smoke. "And he's sixteen?"

"Um, yes."

It wasn't the best time to tell her his birthday was in a month (Leo, I surmised, rehashing zodiac signs in my head and popping little hearts out of my ears). Starry stayed quiet for several minutes. My perception of the situation shifted: from sharing incredible, exciting news to being on trial.

She sighed. She had come to a verdict and was now pondering how much of it to keep to herself and how much to say out loud.

"Listen, Lee, in these things you must make your own mistakes, but I'm unsettled. Let me explain, or better, you tell me. Does it seem normal to you that a sixteen-year-old guy has a crush on an eleven-year-old girl?"

"Twelve, Mom."

"Yeah, okay, twelve in a week, but still I'm worried sick. Girls like Veronica in your class look much older, but you don't."

Ouch!

Mom continued, "I knew you'd have a crush sooner or later, but I was hoping for Flavio or Alex, not a guy that much older. Why isn't he interested in girls his age?"

I had no clue. There weren't any around. I appreciated Mom's honesty though. I answered, "He doesn't seem like a pedophile. He's not creepy or pushy. He's sweet and kind, almost old-fashioned. I have no idea why he likes *me*, but I am so thrilled. Can you be happy for me?"

Starry took a deep breath, then answered, "If I said yes, I'd lie. I'd much rather you'd never see him again." My face blanched. "I'd never force you. But I mean, you didn't even have your first period, yet!"

My cheeks warmed. "Geez, Starry! It's not like I want to make babies at this stage, right?"

Starry did not laugh. "Well, that's great, but he's

sixteen instead, and while I sure hope fatherhood is not in his immediate plans, he didn't ask you to *be together* just to be *friends*, right?"

My mouth opened to retort, but no words came out. Starry added, "Please, please, please, be careful for goodness' sake and don't trust him until you know him *well*. Do nothing you're not one hundred percent comfortable doing, okay?"

"Okay," I promised, my mood dampened. It was as much of a blessing as I would get from Starry.

Now, I had to face Gio.

19

One Second of Happiness

After my sleepless night, I waited till 10 AM to leave the house. The sky was the cloudless, intense blue of a typical June morning, rich with the promise of the heat to come. The air was terse and still fresh; the sun shining in its early summer glory. Droplets of dew persisted in the shadiest corners.

Sonia's Mom answered the door. "Leda, hi, how are you?" She continued in her slow lilt, "I don't know what to do with this girl anymore! She got a second piercing! And last night she came home late, *again*, and she's not studying! At least you're a good influence. Are you still doing well in school?" Overwhelmed by the deluge of words I nodded without elaborating on my very stretched C in English. She carried on, "So help her out, will you?

Go wake her up!"

I got in, knocked at Sonia's bedroom door, and her mom left.

"Mm… *what?*" Sonia protested, her Roman accent more marked than usual. The bed squeaked when she rolled over.

I opened the door and snuck inside. "It's me Sonia! It's half past ten already!"

She sat up, looking concerned in the light filtering from the hallway. "*Lee?* Why are you up so early?"

"I didn't sleep at all." I grinned, closing the door behind me for privacy.

"Oh, Lee, you're such a loser! Were you afraid of vampires?" She mocked me.

"Shitless," I admitted. "You would have been, too, if you *saw* the movie rather than sucking Alex's face, but that's not it."

I walked toward the window, fumbling for the rope to pull the shutters open. I hit my hip into the desk and cursed under my breath. She chuckled.

In the total darkness I could not see Sonia when I said, "Gio asked me!"

"SHUT UP!" She jumped off the bed and shoved me aside to open the shutters. Then she sat back on the bed staring at me, wide awake, her eyebrows arching. She swallowed. "Are you pulling my leg?"

"Nu-uh."

"*Porca merda*! Gio? *The* Gio? *Baywatch*, ripped-abs Gio? Asked *you*?"

Finally the reaction I was expecting. "Yes, dummy. The one I've been dying after since I met him."

"And what did you say?"

"That I had to think about it."

"Good job! Let him wait!" She cheered me on.

"Actually, I was a jerk. He's right. You don't need to think about it if you like someone."

"*Wrong*. It's just the suspense that keeps interest alive. If you say yes, you're done, a thing of the past."

"Well, I'm glad I didn't explain my answer to him like *that*." We both laughed.

Sonia asked, "So, you're gonna say yes?"

"I guess." I looked at the bed sheet.

"What do you mean? Anyone would and you've been dying after him like… forever." She grabbed her green bikini.

"Anyway, enough about me," I replied. "You had a good go with Alex, right?"

Sonia's smile faded. "Yes, but there's no passion, no spark. He's a klutz, too. To be honest, I keep thinking about Martino." She scraped her teeth against her lower lip.

"Yeah, he's quite the sex-symbol," I added gaining a stuffed bear to my face. I added, "So, what are you going to do?"

"I don't know. I might have to break up with Alex."

"If you're sure…"

"Aaaaah! I'm not!" she exploded in frustration.

"Weren't these things were *simple*?" I retorted, quoting Sonia.

"What are you talking about? It's a mess! Can *you* talk to Alex?"

"*Me*? And what am I gonna say?"

"Well, he'll listen to you. If I talk to him what's he gonna do, cry? Neither of us can take it. If you ease him into it…"

"Not even at gunpoint, I'm not. What the hell!"

"Lee, please! You have a way with words, I'm a… not so good. I'll hurt him more, and it'd be a mess. *Please*?"

"Fine." I regretted my answer as soon as the sadness left her face. Sonia was over it, me, I had to break up with Alex.

I stepped on the pool grounds, Sonia beside me. Gio was glorious in his lifeguard chair, so much so I averted my eyes. Alex was on his towel listening to the radio. Every morning his parents woke him up at eight to study for two hours, then he swam laps with Gio as his only witness.

Sonia and I walked through the gate and Gio

greeted us.

"Hi." I said, looking away, trying to act casual and failing, at least judging by the heat rising to my face.

I resolved to escape the emotional intensity of the situation with Gio giving myself bummer time with Alex. I had no choice anyway, since Sonia kept pushing my back whispering in my ear, "Go! Go! Do it! I don't want to talk to Alex before you do!"

I rolled my eyes and walked to Alex. "Yo, we need to talk."

"Great, I sure do," he answered, standing.

"*You* do?"

We passed Gio and sat on the porch of the small building that served as a clubhouse for parties beside the pool. Now everything closed.

The tiled floor chilled my thighs. I asked, "So, what did *you* want to talk about?"

"Well, things with Sonia aren't great." My task would be easier than Sonia had expected. "It's boring. We never talk, *ever*. All she wants to do is suck face, but that's not so great either."

His confession took me by surprise and I tried to regroup. "Ah, right. She has her doubts herself. Maybe it's better if you stay friends?"

"You mean she's dumping me?"

"Ah, yeah."

Alex raised his eyebrows. "And couldn't she tell

me herself?"

I agreed but had to play the devil's advocate. "Yes, but the general hurt situation terrified her so she asked me to intercede."

"*Intercede*?" Alex laughed. "You read a lot, don't you? Well, thank you."

He didn't look happy but took it better than I expected, excavating himself from the stolen-panties pit-of-shame.

"It's better this way," he said standing. "Want to go for a walk?"

"No, sorry. I have to talk to Gio and—"

"To Gio?" he asked as my cheeks sizzled. He added, "Come on, just ten minutes to clear my mind. We'll be right back."

The prospect of leaving Alex in the dumps was awful, and the only other person at the pool, beyond the hot lifeguard of my dreams, was Sonia.

"Fine," I conceded looking at Gio, who was reading oblivious to our presence.

Alex and I strolled around the Pro, and it turned out to be therapeutic. He cracked jokes about my negligible height and soon smiled again. I got angry, but at least relaxed. In fifteen minutes we were back at the pool.

Alex walked me to the gate, then stopped. "I

have a tennis match with my brother, I'll see you later."

"You have a brother?" I asked.

"Yeah. He's a pain in my *culo*. Older, studies all the time, Dad's favorite…"

"Well, if you're the other option…" I winked, moving away.

"I still can fit you in my pocket, Lee!" he yelled after me as we parted.

I walked in.

Gio blurted, "*So*?" He sounded annoyed. He gestured for me to sit at the bottom of his chair, which I did, surprised by his curt tone. He added, "Lee, at least answer me. You've been keeping me hanging long enough, don't you think? If you don't want to be with me say it, and we'll still be friends. You can go run around with Alex l*ater*."

Wow, he *was* jealous! Of *Alex*?

He glared at me, so I said, "But I do. I do want to be with you." I hoped the increasing heat on my face did not match the intensity of my blushing.

"You do?"

I nodded, and he exploded in laughter, hugging me sideways right where I was sitting. I was terrified and happy at the same time. As he let me go, I ran to the towels without looking back, my thoughts in a jumble of periods, babies, and Fahrenheit.

I didn't know what Gio expected from our being

together, but embarrassment overwhelmed me. I felt inadequate, weak, and exposed. I sure was not used to it and did not like it.

"So what did he say?" Sonia asked, as soon as I was within earshot.

"Who, Gio?"

"No, dummy! Alex! Did you dump him? What did he say? And why did you disappear with him for so long?"

I rolled my eyes. "Gee, you guys, it was fifteen minutes, max."

"Was he a wreck?" Sonia asked.

"No, he agreed it was for the best."

Sonia's jaw dropped. "Son of a *puttana*! He didn't care, did he?"

I looked at my friend in disbelief. "Are *you* angry, now? You dumped him! Oh no, actually you didn't. You had *me* do it for you! At least be happy you didn't break his heart!"

"True…but I'm a little disappointed, you know? He seemed so into me two days ago and then it all evaporated into nothing."

I understood her point of view, feeling guilty for setting them up. "Well, I guess it wasn't meant to be."

Oli walked through the gate, cutting our conversation short. Everybody else joined soon after, including Alex, back from the tennis courts. He ignored Sonia and chatted with Klara and me instead. This upset Sonia and caused me to curse her whims.

Oli announced, throwing down his cards, "Fine! All into the water!"

Valerio smirked. "I kicked your *culo*!"

Oli didn't look at him, but answered, "Like I said, all into the water!"

Everyone lined up by the fence as far from the pool as possible. Big, cement squares surrounded the water. I stood on one tile facing off Alex.

"Rock, paper, scissors!" we yelled at once.

My paper lost to his scissors, and I hopped one square closer to the water. Oli and Valerio ran in between us with their arms spread out, humming like planes. They took a hold of Alex and threw him into the water. So much for rock, paper, scissors. They turned around aiming at me while Francesco and Klara scampered away screeching.

"Lifeguard! Lifeguard!" I screamed. "These brutes want to drown me."

Gio shot from his chair and lifted me in his arms. I didn't have time to absorb what was happening since he jumped into the water. Everybody else followed as a spraying and drowning contest started. I was good at it since I had accumulated significant bully experience.

Someone threw a ball. I lined up at the springboard waiting for Francesco to jump. I didn't see Gio sneaking up on me. He came from behind me and stamped a quick kiss on my cheek before going back to his chair.

And that's when the *merda* hit the fan.

20

Consequences

Did someone else see Gio stamping that kiss on my cheek? Why did he do that? What did he want from this, from *me*? Kisses, making out, babies, periods, scratching my palm, a big red bike, soooo much older, Fahrenheit, and a lot of fear. I liked him but could not stand where any of this was going, probably to hell on a train of guilt, judging by Grandma's and Jesus' teachings.

"Sonia. Swings. Now," I whispered to my friend who was moping away watching Alex joke with Klara.

Once we sat on the swings, she was the first one to talk. "Why does Alex ignore me? He looks so hot when he doesn't care for me!"

"YOU'VE GOT TO BE KIDDING ME! *Now*

you like him?"

Sonia shrugged. "More than when we were dating."

"You think more like men than you realize, at least according to your own theories. Sonia, you *don't* like him. You hate he's not drooling all over you. If you were back together, he would bore you in a minute. You're behaving like a spoiled brat. Let the poor kid alone already!"

"Wow. You're right. He is hot though."

"A hunk. Hear me out, instead. I have a serious problem. So, I said yes to Gio—"

"You did? Attagirl!"

"Right, but… It's weird. This whole thing makes me anxious, ashamed."

"Of what?"

"Of being somebody's girlfriend, I guess. I don't want to be anybody's. I want no one entitled to do things to me."

"Like what?" Sonia stared, wide-eyed.

"Like *anything*! He gave me a kiss on the cheek, for example."

"Big deal," Sonia said. "Although if it were from Gio—"

"I'm not ready for any of this."

Nun! Nico's words echoed in my brain. Was he right? Would I end up marrying Jesus for real?

"So?" Sonia uttered, dumbfounded.

"So… I must break up with him."

"Are you *stupid*?"

I did not answer, scraping my toes against the dirt below my swing.

Sonia smirked. "So we're not so different; as soon as you got what you wanted it became old hat, huh?"

I frowned. "*What*? No way! You didn't get what you wanted."

"What do you mean?"

"You want Martino, Sonia, but he's ten and you can't get him. I, instead, really got what I wanted, but I can't handle it. It's like… Gio, who got his bike before his license. He cannot ride it, yet."

Sonia laughed. "Yeah, don't ride Gio, quite yet. And anyway, he does ride his bike, in the Pro at least."

"You're missing my point!" I answered, giving her the stink-eye.

Sonia glared back. "*You* are missing my point, Lee! It's not like Gio is gonna throw away his bike because he has no license, *yet*, but this is what you're doing. No offense, but you're a pretty fucked-up kid. You're moody, nerdy, happy, angry, sad. Nobody ever knows what's going on into that brain of yours! You're short, flat, twelve, and you got this gorgeous looking seventeen-year-old after you, and what do you do? You dump his sorry *culo* after one hour because he gave you a peck on the cheek?"

She was right, yet I couldn't change the emptiness and loneliness inside of me as if the rush of feelings that had flooded me in the past few days had taken everything that was the old Lee away leaving nothing in its place.

I returned to the towels, put my clothes on, and went home without saying goodbye to anyone.

I could not bear to talk to Gio, but I couldn't be with him either. The consideration of how badly I had judged Sonia a few hours earlier for not having the guts to break up with Alex caused me a bitter smile. I picked up a pen and a piece of paper and I wrote the letter that would let Gio down.

"Dear Gio,

I would never tell you these things in person without making a mess. I like you a lot, but I am not ready to be with anyone, and this situation makes me uncomfortable. Can we remained friends? I'm very sorry and I hope you understand.

I really care for you,

Leda"

I put my pen down and cried.

That evening, Gio came to pick me up with his flaming red bike and a winning smile. I felt stupid and guilty, and I wanted to go back to bored and aloof as soon as possible. Eyes on my feet, I skirted around him to give him an awkward peck on the cheek without getting too close. Funny how I would have kissed anyone else to greet them with no hesitation.

He asked, "What's wrong?"

We walked side by side, him pushing his bike, at least till the curve.

"I wrote you a letter," I confessed, voice trembling. I pulled out from my pocket the piece of paper folded in four that read: "4 Gio".

"Thank you," he said, smiling and oblivious. To my horror, he put it away in his own jeans.

I panicked. "No, please read it now."

He hesitated. "Okay, but first hop on."

I enjoyed the thirty-seconds of what could have been our last ride together. As we reached the tennis courts, I sought comfort among the familiar faces of my friends. Gio sat by himself, reading the letter. I also sat by myself, devoured by anxiety. Alex arrived and crouched beside me.

"All alone?" he asked.

"Kinda," I answered, looking at Gio. I should have stopped by Sonia's, since she wasn't out yet.

Alex poked my side, cracking stupid jokes. He was such a dumb, young kid, like myself. Everything about him was ordinary and comfortable.

Gio stood up and walked to us. His face was dark, his forehead wrinkled, and his eyes as intense as glowing embers. I flinched while Alex stared at him, then at me.

"Hi, Gio," Alex said, ill at ease, but Gio ignored him staring at me, and motioning with his head for me to follow him.

I got up, reluctant to suffer the consequences of my actions. He had scared me enough when he was happy, now everything inside me shook, as if an internal windstorm picked up because of his rage.

At first he tried to smile. "Lee, listen, I understand that our age difference might intimidate you, but it's not like I want to jump your bones." I cringed, and he added, "I'm chill, and I will never, in the most absolute way, do anything you don't want me to."

"So, we're friends?"

"Let's not make a drama out of this. We can be together and that's that, with no consequences."

"So, what's the point?"

I felt trapped, pushed into something I wasn't ready for, and I hated it. He looked bitter, and I felt sorry but breaking up was the right choice. As much as I liked Gio, he terrified me with his jealousy and anger, and I needed distance between us.

"Is this your last word?" he asked.

I nodded with no doubt, only regret.

Gio turned around and hopped on his bike. The last thing I had wanted was to hurt him and yet, here we were. Nico was right, sometimes you had to hurt the people you cared about.

I wanted to stop Gio, stop his pain, be what he needed me to be, but instead I was just me. I watched him through tears as he skidded away, leaving *way* too fast.

Jesus, please keep him safe… please, please, please. I recited in my head while swallowing hard sitting back on the sidewalk by Alex, who looked at me aghast and asked, "What the hell happened?"

"Nothing," I answered, picturing myself dissolving into the wind like smoke.

"*Nothing*? Well, that *nothing* seemed *intense*. Where did Gio go?"

I shrugged. "For a ride?"

"Is there something going on between you two?"

"No." I stared right ahead of me in the darkness. "We're just friends."

On Wednesday, Italy was to play Uruguay for the round of sixteen of the *Italia 90* world cup. I did not care much for soccer, but I still knew the teams, better players, and game results, which was inevitable unless you lived in a cave.

Yet, for *Italia 90* we were meant to win the cup that bore our name. God wanted it and to this end had sent Totò Schillaci. Totò had been good enough to make the team but was on the second string. He had subbed during the first game and scored within two minutes. He had not stopped scoring since, shining with the light of the divine champion Italians believed he was.

Sonia and I showed up late. Everyone was in Oli's living room, except Gio. I had seen him at the pool, in his usual chair, reading his books and ignoring me, but he hadn't been around in the evenings since our breakup four days ago.

Sonia sat on the floor, beside Martino, and I scooted by Oli's couch. I checked the faces of the friends who had suffered because of love. Alex and Francesco cheered players exchanging high fives. Martino gazed on, impassible, while Sonia threw him side-glances. Klara, who cheered for Germany, had agreed to Italy as her second favorite team and chatted with Laura. Everyone seemed fine. I, after four whole days, was still in shambles. I had barely slept since the stupid vampire movie, and I had a hole in my chest that had leaked out any hope, joy, or energy.

Who's the drama queen now?

GOAL!

Schillaci scored at the sixty-fifth minute. I wanted to belong, so I screamed as loud as I could, not for happiness, but to get rid of the frustration, loneliness, and sadness I had accumulated since Saturday, or since my parents had split, or since I had begun to unravel this whole girl thing: it sucked.

It didn't matter why, but I drowned my pain in the screaming and yelling, getting high on everybody else's adrenaline and excitement, losing myself in the fever of the world cup. That's the beauty of sport fanaticism, it lets you get excited and drugged up with everybody else's emotions when you have none left into your own gray life. I leaned on that false sense of belonging to anesthetize my thoughts and pretended that what mattered was that we had qualified for the quarterfinals.

My birthday would surprise me big time.

21

Forever Yours

On Saturday I opened my eyes, blinking a couple of times as I realized that Starry was calling me from downstairs.

I sat on my bed and Sonia walked into my bedroom screaming, "Happy Birthday, Lee! You're twelve! Come on, Oli's waiting in the foyer," she said smiling.

"*Oli*? What—*why*?"

She shrugged. I slid into my usual pool outfit and dragged myself downstairs.

"Happy Birthday, Lee!" Oli exclaimed, presenting me with a wrapped package.

"For me? Thank you!"

Everyone had signed the card, except Gio. I opened the gift to find a gigantic t-shirt advertising

Oli's father's company. The gesture moved me nonetheless. "Thank you guys, that's, um, sweet."

I wore the t-shirt that reached to my knees and headed out for the pool with my friends. The weather was overcast.

Really, Jesus? Clouds on my birthday?

It felt personal. I explained to Jesus in my head why it was important that it'd be sunny and a sunbeam broke through. I smiled, thanking him in my head.

I walked right past Gio sitting in his chair.

"Hi," I said. He ignored me, like he had for a week.

I sighed and lay on my towel, put Vasco on my Walkman, and annihilated my sad thoughts into waves of music. Vasco sang *Ogni Volta, Every Time*. It comforted me to know Vasco was lonely, too, and overwhelmed by his own mistakes. Despite Vasco and the screeching of Sonia playing cards with Martino I fell into a deep slumber to recoup the sleep stolen by vampires and my broken heart.

That night at the tennis courts I heard the sound of a familiar motorbike and lost track of Sonia's chatter. Gio parked, dismounted from his ride, and took a quick glance at the Company, making a bee-line for *me*.

"Uh oh," Sonia said.

If she had noticed, it must have been obvious. Was he still mad?

He stopped right in front of me. I was bewildered, torn between the hope of a reconciliation and the fear of further hostilities.

I smiled. "Hello?"

He hesitated, opened his mouth, then froze. He tilted his head sideways, a gestured I recognized. His expression was sweeter as if his anger had dissolved, or so I hoped. He handed me a white envelope, sealed.

"Read it at home," he said.

I nodded and put it in the pocket of my denim jacket, but for the whole evening I thought of nothing else.

As soon as I got home, I drank cherry juice to calm my nerves. The paper weighed in my pocket with its mysterious contents. The opportunity to communicate with Gio caused a buzz in my head, but I preferred to dwell in my ignorance where I hoped that the letter was not hurtful and full of the rage that had drained from his eyes.

I walked to the living room, where Viola sat in front of the TV, watching Video Music Channel. I wanted to connect with her, to tell her of my heartache.

I said, "Isn't Vasco's song *Ogni Volta* beautiful?"

Viola didn't turn and answered, "Just the rambling of a drug addict."

Again, I had misunderstood everything.

Once upstairs I brushed my teeth, put on my pajamas, and sat on the bed in the familiar spotlight of my bedside lamp: the peculiar and introspective stage of many sleepless nights. Here I had experienced extreme joy, excitement, fear, anxiety, loneliness, and sometimes anger. But the sad pang piercing my chest, the loss and ineluctability were new. I did not understand what was wrong, but my mistake must have been egregious judging by its consequences. Silence pressed, boring, waiting for content.

I took a deep breath and tore the envelope. For the first time, I saw Gio's handwriting, neat and grown-up, but the realization there was more in the envelope overcame my surprise. I turned it upside down and caught in my hand a thin golden necklace with a small pendant in the shape of a heart and a tiny red stone. My breath sped up while I held back the tears. I opened the letter and read,

"Dear Leda,

I am very sorry that things didn't work out between us, but I respect your choice. Keep this necklace to remind you of me. Happy Birthday!

Yours always,

Gio"

Wow.

I read it and reread it as more tears blurred his words.

How I could keep the necklace forever, like a cross marking the loss of a loved one, to remind me of the pain rotting in my chest? I *wanted* to forget, and I did not want Gio to be *mine forever*. I wanted him to be happy and to go back to friends like before, but how?

The next day at the pool Roberto, the real lifeguard, filled what had been Gio's chair for two weeks. My mood precipitated even lower. Wow, two weeks was a long time, an eternity. I felt older, so much older, and excited to leave for vacation in one more day. Time to change pace, place, and face, too. I smirked at my silly pun as I joined the Company, sprawled on the grass. Gio was nowhere in sight. After two hours, I picked up my courage and went to his house.

"Yes?" his mother asked, frigid as ever. She didn't like me, and at the moment I agreed with her.

"Ah, good afternoon, ma'am. Is Gio home?"

"He's studying."

"Can I talk to him for a minute?" She stared. I added, "Just one minute, I promise. I don't want to distract him from his studies, I need to—" I was going to say *give him something*, but she could have done that. "Ah, I wanted to ask him one quick thing." She still stared. I added, "*Please*?"

"One minute, no more."

She disappeared without inviting me in. When Gio came at the door, he looked surprised to see me. "Lee?"

"Ah, hi."

"What's up?" He reached me at the gate. "Let's go sit in the shade."

"Ah, sure," I answered. What the hell was I thinking? This was my worst idea, yet.

We sat side by side on the sidewalk across the street till I uttered, "Gio, I—" I tried to look at him and ended up checking my shoes instead. "I wanted to thank you for your thought." I showed him the envelope where I had put back the necklace.

"Well, it was your birthday."

"Yes, but—" I sighed. "I can't keep it." He opened his mouth to protest, but I stopped him with my hand. "No, listen. It's too much. I'm so sorry that things didn't work out, too, but this is yours, not mine."

I put it in his hand and I did what I could do best; I ran away.

Ten days before I would have died rather than go on vacation, but now I couldn't wait. I was more like Sonia than I had thought.

I spent the rest of the afternoon at the pool making friendship bracelets, the latest fad in the Company. We created patterns with cotton, knots, and creativity, coming up with new designs.

The boys splashed in the water, and Sonia kept chattering about Martino, "…I know he's only ten, but he's sooo cute! Isn't he, Klara?"

Klara answered, "Mm, quite the mysterious type." She knotted away.

"He sure has secrets," Sonia added, giggling at her private joke and messing up her bracelet since she was a klutz.

Klara looked at me and asked, "Lee, are you okay?"

"Who *me*? Yeah, peachy." I sounded so awful I couldn't have convinced even Sonia. They both looked at me, so I added, "Sorry, I— It's nothing."

Sonia's face lit up with excitement. "Don't tell me you broke up with Gio!"

She knew freaking well I had but wanted to look smart in front of Klara. Klara did not flinch but gave me an encouraging smile. Sonia has probably gossiped to her about Gio and I to some extent. I didn't even care.

"I'm sorry, Lee," Klara said. "What happened?"

I answered, "Nothing, just me being a dork. I think he's too old for me and I… freaked, I guess."

"Well, then it was not meant to be. Take it easy, okay?"

Klara's kindness moved me since I was so used to Sonia's insensitive remarks. To hold back the tears I nodded and focused on my bracelet, wishing it broke once I'd be ready for my first kiss. Likely, never.

"Tell Klara about the necklace," Sonia prodded, giving away that she had known about the breakup for a while. I complied, wanting Klara's opinion on my reaction.

Alex startled me by saying in English, "*Much ado about nothing.*"

The three of us turned, startled, and I protested, "What the hell, dude! Not your business! How much did you hear?"

"Enough," he answered.

I frowned. "And what did you say?"

"It's Shakespeare. It means much fuss about nothing. I know the necklace. It comes as a freebie in the *Dash.*"

"The what?" Klara asked.

"Dash," I answered, "It's a laundry detergent."

"*Really*?" Sonia asked, smirking.

"Oh, yeah," Alex answered. "Thin, golden color with a little red stone, that's the one."

"So what?" I asked. "What does it matter? He gave it to *me*!"

"Well," Alex's eyes were stern. "I guess he didn't think you were worth much. I'm glad you returned it."

"Gee, take it easy…" I replied.

Alex and Gio had never liked each other much, but Alex's reaction was overboard. He was being overprotective, but I did not mind. At least *some* friends had my back. It was time to go on vacation. The best summer of my life had only just began.

PART 3

22

An Italian Summer

The morning I was to leave for summer camp in Tuscany was as gloomy and stagnant as my mood. A gray, compact sky weighed on our little *Panda* car, trudging through the still city as if it were a very warm glass globe without snow.

The early hour made the experience surreal since nothing moved and no one was around at least till *Piazza Castello*, where two big *Broggi* buses buzzed like giant bee-hives. Moms, teenagers, and luggage colored the empty streets filling the sky with noise.

"Okay, here we are." Starry sighed. "Will you be okay?"

I rolled my eyes. "Yes, Mom."

"It's only for two weeks anyway. Call me as soon

as you get there, okay?"

"Mom, I'll see what I can do."

"Seriously!"

I huffed. "Starry, as soon as I find a phone, I'll call you. I'm sure if something happened they would get in touch."

"Don't even *say* that!" She looked at me teary-eyed as if I was going to war rather than summer camp, but her weakness made me stronger. She continued, "And remember, the second week I'll be away with Marco, but you can always call Grandma in Afes or your father, understood?" We hugged, and she asked, "I can't park here, are you gonna manage with the luggage?"

"Yes, just go now. I'll be fine." I dragged my suitcase out of the car, hoping it was true.

Once on the bus, I scanned the kids, forcing myself to sit by someone I liked, which was a big change from picking an empty seat. Enough letting fate screw with me!

"Is anyone sitting here?" I asked, trying my best smile.

A brunette with smooth hair to her shoulders smiled back. "No, all yours."

"Leda." I offered my hand.

"Mara."

I sat and hung my small backpack on the hook of the seat in front of me.

"How old are you?" Mara asked.

"Twelve, you?"

"Fifteen, almost."

She would have been perfect for Gio.

She continued, "First time in summer camp?"

"Yep. You?"

"Yeah." She was chewing on her nails. "It's weird to be on my own."

No matter how scared I was, my first instinct was to make Mara feel better. I looked around the packed bus and said, "Well, we're not by ourselves. Are we?"

"I guess not!" She laughed. "Have you ever been in Tuscany?" I shook my head, and she continued, "Me neither. Although we won't see much. From what I understood we'll spend the week in the forest. At least I will. I chose the adventure camp."

"No way! Me too!"

"That's awesome! Can we ask to be roommates?"

"That sounds great!" I grinned.

We chatted the whole way south. Mara had finished her second year of high school, the classic-letters curriculum, and said Latin and Greek were hard. Starry hoped in two years I would choose the same path, but there was no way in hell. It sounded boring. Mara didn't deny it.

The bus left the highway, plunging in a thicket of trees that only grew taller and denser. We wound uphill, and passed a sign that read, *Ciocco Ragazzi, ecology, sport and adventure*.

We disembarked at the information center, and Mara and I followed our group to a smaller van.

In no time, we were settling in our bungalow with two more girls, at least judging by the number of cots and numerous items strewn around the otherwise bare, cavernous bunker. There was no electricity.

The door slammed open.

"Hello!" said a gorgeous girl, huge brown eyes and the thickest braid I had ever seen. "Welcome to my realm. I am Lisa."

A second girl pushed her inside, adding, "Don't listen to her *stronzate*, she's full of it, but she's nice!" They tumbled in, looked at each other and laughed.

The second girl straightened. She had short black hair and bright blue eyes, freckles covering her face. "My name is Francesca and this one here is Queen Lisa," she said while her friend bowed to us.

"Ah, hi. I'm Leda."

"And I'm Mara. I hope we won't be spending too much time in *here*, right?"

Francesca answered, "Not at all. Believe me, if Queen Lisa made it for a week, so can you." Lisa punched her arm.

"So you've been here for a week already? How is it?" I asked.

Lisa answered, "We had a blast! Today is our favorite day so far, because there are no activities, and we've been scanning the new arrivals to find the hottest boy on the grounds. Come on! We'll show you around."

We dropped our bags and followed the two friends outside. As we left, a dazzling sun blinded us.

"Wow! The sun came out!" I exclaimed, taking in the hillside where ten identical bungalows lined up.

Lisa gestured ahead of us. "… And here is the clubhouse, where we all get together when it rains, hopefully never, and where we eat."

Outside the clubhouse many picnic tables littered the lawn. The whole settlement was nestled in the side of a hill, in the middle of a lush forest of poplars, oaks, and chestnut trees. The sun weaved in and out of them carving lacy patterns on the grass. Around us, taller knolls quivered with thick vegetation. Green surrounded us, and I loved it. We sat at one of the picnic tables, perusing the crowd of newcomers and veterans mingling, shaking hands, and making their way to the bungalows. The van kept unloading more.

I pointed at the end of the lawn, where two

grown-ups were sweating, putting up a big white screen. "What are they doing up there?"

Francesca's blue eyes lit up with excitement. "It's for the game! Quarterfinals tonight, Ireland-Italy!"

"Go *Italia*!" I yelled, shaking my fist in the air.

Lisa joked, "Wow! We have a true hooligan here! Your mom must be so worried letting you run amok like this!"

I jumped up. "Geez, speaking of which, where is the phone?" Lisa pointed at the clubhouse and I ran to call.

After dinner the whole summer camp gathered in front of the big screen. We knew we would win and just anticipated the adrenaline and the joy. It was around 9 PM, yet the day was still dimming into dusk.

Queen Lisa slapped her arm. "Freaking mosquitos!"

Francesca said, "Put more bug spray on, Lisa. No one will smell you, I promise."

"I'd rather die bloodless!"

I chimed in, "Oh come on, there are barely any mosquitos here. The breeze keeps them at bay."

Lisa whined, "That's because they're all *on me*."

"Seriously," Francesca added, "Where are you from, Lee, the jungle?"

"Ah, Milan," I answered showing them my ankles swollen with bites, and cursing the muggy Po Valley under my breath. "And you?"

"Torino."

"Aosta."

Everyone's response came at once just when the familiar electric guitar introduced *Un'Estate Italiana, An Italian Summer*, the opening theme of the FIFA cup. The tune slowed as Bennato and Gianna Nannini sang about magical nights spent chasing a goal under the sky of an Italian summer. I loved the song to the point it always gave me goose bumps.

As soon as the refrain picked up, everyone sang along in the biggest choir I had been a part of. Nobody cared that I was off key. It was amazing. Fifty or sixty people, gathered in a forest in the middle of nowhere, swayed in the breeze, singing with no restraint about our relentless will to win and the best Italian summer ever.

When the song ended, we exploded in a mad applause, screaming, cheering. Someone chanted, "Schi-lla-ci, Schi-lla-ci!" and everyone picked it up so loud we drowned the commentator.

At the thirty-eighth minute Totò Schillaci ran, dribbled, and scored. The lawn exploded.

Everyone jumped up at once, clapping hands and screaming as loud as they could, exchanging high fives and hugging perfect strangers. This man, who had started as a sub, would win the golden trophy solo. I wished I could be like him one day, the underdog, the unlikely hero.

In the general mayhem, I noticed two kids in front of us turning one-hundred-and-eighty degrees to glance at us and then whisper to each other giggling.

"Do I have something on my face?" I wondered out loud, belligerent, to no one in particular, hoping they would stop.

Lisa whispered, "No, dummy! That's Damiano!" She adjusted a perfect bang behind her perfect ear. "We met him today while you and Mara went to call home."

That made sense. Damiano and his friend weren't looking at *me*. I blushed, hoping they hadn't heard my comment. Yet, once the crowd quieted, they turned.

The blond one asked, "How goes it, Lisa?" He reminded me of Alex, but his eyes were of a piercing blue so bright to be obvious even in the flickering light of the big screen.

"Hey, Damiano! These are our roomies," Lisa gestured at us, "Leda and Mara."

"Um, Leda, the *feisty* one," he said with a huge grin, while I held up his gaze. He motioned at his friend, "This hunk here is Stefano, my wingman."

Stefano rolled his eyes. "Please forgive my silly friend, he doesn't know what he's saying."

I liked Stefano's composed yet funny demeanor. With jet-black hair and dark eyes, he was the antithesis of Damiano. I smiled and shook his hand, then Damiano's. Mara did the same. The game reserved no more surprises, and Italy qualified to the semi-finals.

After the game Mara, Lisa, Fra, and I lay in our cots in the dark, our flashlights close.

Lisa declared out of context, "Damiano is hot!" Everyone giggled.

Mara said, "He sure is. How old is he?"

Queen Lisa answered, "Fourteen, one year older than me. Perfect match." More giggling.

Mara asked, "What do you think, Lee?"

"Not my type," I answered. Hooting noises came from all over the bungalow.

Francesca asked, "And what's your type like, oh, tough cookie?"

"Mm…" I described Gio, butterflies fluttering in my stomach. I added, "At least I *think* that's my type."

"Sounds good," Lisa said.

"Sounds like Stefano," Francesca added.

"What do you mean *I think*?" Mara asked.

I sighed. "It's complicated." I explained how I had ditched the man of my dreams.

Mara said, "Sometimes it's a matter of chemistry. Someone might have all the characteristics you think are important, but if it doesn't click, it just doesn't."

I answered, exasperated by my own words, "Oh, but it clicked all right!"

At the same time Francesca asked, "Ha, and what does Mara know about chemistry?"

Mara answered, "One thing at the time. Lee, what the hell did you do, then?"

"Well, he was too old for me, and I freaked out."

"How old?" Lisa asked, sounding all business.

"Seventeen."

"*Porca vacca*!" was more or less the general shocked reaction.

Mara sounded hesitant when she asked, "Did he want you to do something you didn't?"

"No, hell no." I laughed at my stupidity before explaining, "We never got that far. We were together for two hours, he kissed me on the cheek, I freaked out, and that was that."

Lisa asked in the general chuckling, "So, you've kissed no one?"

"Why, did *you*?" I retorted without denying my lack of experience.

"Oh, I sure did! Last year at the seaside. It was

aaaa-wesome! And you, Mara?"

Mara sighed. "Yeah…"

"Uh-oh," Francesca said. "That doesn't sound good. What happened?"

Mara stayed silent too long, dampening the mood.

I murmured, "You okay?"

"Yes," her voice wavered, "It's just that, well, I was with this guy for four months and a half, and I really liked him."

"Oh no! Did the jerk break your heart?" Lisa asked, just as I said,

"Four months and half? That's like, *forever*!"

"Yeah, it was a while. And he did kinda break my heart. He wanted more than kissing, and I wasn't ready. So he broke up with me."

"What a *stronzo*!" Francesca exclaimed.

"Right?" Mara sounded better.

"Right!" I confirmed. "Screw being uncomfortable, screw guys!"

"Yeah, right!" Lisa chuckled as everyone joined her, realizing my unfortunate choice of words.

Mara asked, "What about you, Francesca, kissed anyone?"

I imagined her smirking just by hearing her playful tone. "You betcha I did, and it wasn't special at all. Am I not normal?"

Lisa huffed. "I don't know what to tell you, Fra, kissing was awesome for me."

I answered, "If it helps, Fra, my best friend also didn't like it when she made out with this kid she kind of liked. But when she kissed somebody else by mistake, she was blown away. So, maybe, it's just a matter of kissing the right boy."

"How do you kiss someone *by mistake*?" Mara asked as everyone laughed.

"CURFEW! CURFEW!" A violent knocking on our door shut us up and soon enough regular breathing surrounded me.

"Dear Jesus, thank you so much for sending some cool girls my way. Please help me forget Gio, if you can, and make everyone happy with good reason. Amen."

Jesus was about to surprise me big time.

23

Semi-finals

On the night of the semi-finals, Italy played Argentina, one of our most hated enemies; nothing to do with the country, actually. The hate of most, surely mine, focused against their captain: Diego Maradona, who had been leading Naples in the Italian league since I could remember. People adored him like a god in the southern city. They had little altars with his picture, flowers, and candles, and they *prayed* to him, among many other saints they venerated and killed chickens for.

Italy is Catholic to the bone, but superstition and the passion for soccer run as deep, meeting in the strange Maradona cult. I disliked the sleazy character. Involved in several scandals with cocaine and hookers, he had scored with a hand in the previous world cup against England in a forgiven handling foul baptized as *the hand of God*. I could have gotten over all of this, but playing against Italy, almost his own country, was unforgivable.

I sat on one of the many folding chairs spread on the lawn and stared bewildered at the huge screen. A good number of fans at the game cheered for Argentina. Signs in Italian celebrated Maradona and his team.

I asked, “How is this possible?”

Stefano, sitting beside us with his friend Damiano, answered, “Well, the game is taking place in Naples, and a lot of the locals chose their hero over their nation.”

“But it’s treason!”

Everyone agreed. The whole thing made me more eager to win the freaking game.

It didn’t take long. At the seventeenth minute, Schillaci scored: Un-be-lie-vable! The crowd was the loudest ever.

Everyone chanted the classic, “Alé-oh-oh,” while making the wave around our little crowd.

Argentina's goal at the sixty-seventh was a backstabbing. Dino, a staff guy in his twenties, turned around and yelled at us, in his strong Tuscan accent that made harsh sounds pronounced as Hs, “Oh good God you’re all so quiet now, are you? Make them hear you in Naples!”

We screamed and chanted, but the game ended 1-1 and moved to penalty kicks. Both teams would shoot five times, only the shooter and the goalie to face each other. Whoever scored the most, won.

It was our cup, in Italy, and God wanted us to win. We had been playing fair and at an outstanding level. Argentina… not so much with four yellow cards and a red one. Yet a sliver of doubt made me fearful enough to have my stomach up in knots.

A kid sitting in the row behind us said, "Zenga is the best goalie in the whole world cup. They don't stand a chance."

Lisa turned around. "Shhhhh! Don't jinx it!"

Goal after goal, we ended up 3-3 and then, Donadoni missed his chance.

Maradona didn't.

Serena, our last chance, shot right into the goalie.

We were out of our own world cup. We hadn't won. Maradona had.

Italy lost *Italia 90* and it had never been so quiet, I bet. A few kids cried and hugged but most crawled back to their bungalows. No final, no more magical nights, no more Italian summer. End of the adventure. The world cup was over.

The second week in Tuscany was but a shadow of

the first since Mara, Damiano and Stefano had left. I was stuck in a movie after the end. The main characters were gone and the world cup was lost forever, but I was still stuck in Tuscany. I didn't mingle with the newcomers, striking instead a friendship with Dino, the Tuscan staff member.

Lisa joked, "You have a thing for old dudes, huh?"

"Hell no. I don't like Dino that way, *at all.*"

"Yeah, yeah, yeah," she answered walking away.

I didn't get it. Couldn't I as a girl be a person in my own right without being tacked on a random male? Did I *have to* like someone and be liked back? Because so far, I sucked at both.

Wednesday was bonfire night.

We took off from the adventure camp base at dusk, wading through the woods full of mosquitos and other invisible, scuttling creatures. As always, when on the move, someone sang. Unfortunately the racist song ranted against people from Naples.

"*Napoli merda, Napoli colera,*
Sei la rovina dell'Italia intera
Napoletani, terremotati,
Che col sapone non si sono mai lavati…"

It went on and on, catchy because it rhymed. Was I angry with some people from Naples because of their behavior during the world cup? Yes, very much, but this was *not* acceptable, not to mention that the Irpinia earthquake dated to 1980, and regardless it should not have been cause of mockery. Only Grandma and a few elders thought God was behind it.

I blurted in frustration, mostly to my friends, "Oh, *come on*!"

A kid ahead of me snapped back his head. "*What*? Are *you* from Naples? You like Maradona?"

"No, dude, mind your own business."

He glared at me. "Well, *stronza*, *you* didn't. So what, are you a *sympathizer*?"

Ouch!

He acted so dumb, I lost it. "Listen up," I said. "I hate that Italians cheered against Italy at the cup, but at least they cheered for the wrong country rather than hating their own! And whoever was at the game in Naples is not *here* to hear your stupid songs!"

A bunch of kids exclaimed, "Woooooo!"

I did not see it coming; the the racist kid slapped my face with all of his might, hitting me square in the jaw. It hurt like hell and my ear whistled. Tears welled up at the corner of my eyes, but I didn't cry. Instead, my evil side took over so violently I didn't even realize it as I chased the stupid ass to kill him. I would hit him so hard he wo*uld* cry, but he ran faster. I had been an unbeatable runner before puberty but not anymore.

I stopped running, bent over double to catch my breath. My head echoed with the ring of the unfair slap, my face hot with heat, but what hurt most was my massive anger folding onto itself, turning into humiliation.

Lisa and Francesca caught up with me. Francesca asked, "Are you okay?"

"Yeah," I lied.

"Who-hoo!" Lisa yelled giving me a hug. "You sure told that *stronzo* off! I can't believe he ran away! *Chicken*!" she screamed toward the head of the column.

A girl walked up to me. "Thank you," she said. "I *am* from Naples, and that was awesome."

I blushed. For once Mr. Hyde had accomplished something good.

When we made it to the big lawn, huge bonfires burned the night and their smoky scent filled my nostrils. Several other groups were already there: volleyball, basketball, who knew what else. In spite of Lisa's words, the episode in the woods had left me with a lingering sting on my face and an odd melancholy: I didn't belong.

Dino handed me a sprig. "Here you go, Lee." He explained, "These heather sticks don't burn well and we use them to roast marshmallows. They're hard to find, so don't throw them in the fire."

I shrugged. "Marshmallows are perfect, no need to roast them," I said stuffing a couple in my mouth.

He laughed. "Because you didn't try. It's the American way."

I wasn't listening anymore. Ensnared by the ever-changing, glowing embers, I enjoyed the soothing heat.

Dino asked, out of nowhere, "Are you sad?"

He took me by surprise since he did not seem like the introspective type.

I rushed to answer, "Of course not!" Nobody likes a downer. Sonia had told me so many times and Mom had taught me that no matter how bad life got, the correct answer was that *everything is okay*.

He kept staring, unconvinced, so I added, "I miss Mara."

"And Stefano," he added.

"Who?"

"Come on, I know you liked him."

"Dino, I didn't—"

He interrupted me. "Oh, don't worry. Mara told me that everyone liked Damiano, but Stefano was more your type."

I sighed. Who cared what Dino thought? Adults: always ready to draw their own conclusions, eager to show they knew better. I was sick and tired of people telling me how I felt when most of the times I had no clue myself.

At least, as long as he thought I pined for Stefano, I could look forlorn in Dino's eyes. I sighed and let my thoughts dissolve into the sky like smoke: dark, but thin and light, becoming one with the night and turning into stars.

Thursday night, I was about to fall asleep into the darkness of our bungalow. A new girl had taken Mara's place, or at least her bed, but our conversations lacked. Someone knocked on the door well after curfew. We were not talking so that staff members would have no reason to bother us.

Lisa mumbled, "Oh, God. Did something happen?"

The new girl slumbered away. The knocking resumed, more urgent.

Francesca got up to open the door. "Let me check."

An unknown male voice violated the intimacy of our dark lair. "Ah, hi. I—, I… Sorry to bother you. My name is Matteo and… is Leda here?"

I jumped in my bed.

Me? What the hell?

Francesca asked, "Isn't it past curfew?"

The boy answered, "Ah, yeah. I'd appreciate it if

you called her."

"Sure, Lee?" she said turning toward the darkness. I saw only her silhouette against the moonlight. I scuttled to the door, and I found myself face to face with a perfect stranger.

24

A Night Visitor

The kid was several inches taller than me, his hair cropped short. The moon, enormous, was shining behind him. It was almost full.

"Hi?" I studied his silhouette.

He took my wrist with urgency. "Hi, I'm Matteo and I have to talk to you, but if we stay here we're gonna get caught. Can you come for a minute?"

Was he a friend of the racist kid? Would he hurt me?

"*We*? Where?" I asked pointing my flip-flops to the ground.

"Just around the corner, out of the moonlight and Dino's patrolling."

Indeed, my friends and Dino were a quick shout away. "Okay," I conceded.

I stepped outside, and he led me toward the back of the bungalow, by the hillside. The hair on my neck was standing on edge. He turned to face me and the moonlight shone on his regular features, two huge eyes, brown or hazel, looking at me. He didn't seem angry or belligerent. He must be one of Lisa's many fans, asking for me to intercede. I relaxed. He put a hand on my arm to steer me along the side of the bungalow, toward the back.

"Have we met?" I whispered.

"I was hoping you would remember me."

Intriguing: who the hell was this mystery kid? We had never spoken. We sat on the grass behind the bungalow, away from the path in front of the cabins. He sighed, as if preparing for a confession. I loved that, for once, I had nothing at stake, nothing to hide, nothing to be ashamed of.

Apparently, *he* did.

He said, "Leda, I— I mean, it's too bad you did not notice me since I— well, I've noticed *you* quite a bit."

Me? This kid noticed me?

He continued, "You've got nothing to say?"

I shook my head, bewildered, unsure of where this was going. I hoped he had a good reason to get me in trouble.

He looked at the grass. We were on a gentle slope and his arms hung loose around his knees. He brought up his hands to rub his face. "Look, this is not… me. I—don't even know where to start, but I owe this to myself. I have a huge crush on you. There, I said it."

He turned towards me. I was still staring, astonished, sure this was a joke. Dino must have been on it too, which explained why Matteo had taken his chances after curfew. Why would a complete stranger want to make fun of me?

Since I blinked, he kept talking, "I'm leaving tomorrow. I have to leave a day early to go to the seaside with my family and I— I finally got the courage to come and talk to you."

I waited for the joke.

The crickets sang, drunk on summer, and fireflies lit the night. They reminded me of the one I had seen in Arese when Gio had asked me to be his girlfriend, except that now I had my wits about me. The magic was outside not inside of me.

I looked at Matteo. "You're kidding me, right? I'd better go back."

He radiated excitement as he held my arm and replied, "It sounds crazy and I'm leaving tomorrow and I'll never see you again, but I've never felt this way before and—Well… I came here to ask you for a kiss."

I scoffed. Dino would come out any moment now.

"Listen, Matteo, you sure are crazy, big time. Like hell I will kiss you. Are we done?" The smile disappeared from Matteo's face, replaced by hurt. My grin froze.

Is he for real?

I continued, "It's *not funny*. You're making me uncomfortable, and I'd rather go to sleep."

"Leda, I swear to God, I'm serious. I'd never joke on something so serious as people's feelings, especially *my own*. I'm an idiot, but I had to talk to you. I— I think you're amazing."

As he stared at the moon from our hiding spot, I could tell that his big eyes were hazel. He didn't know I would never kiss a stranger after having turned down the man of my dreams, yet I admired his fearlessness. If this wasn't a joke, I wished that I could be like him, one day.

I added, "Matteo, sorry if I was rude. You would agree that what you're saying is hard to believe. How can you tell that I'm amazing? We have never spoken. I'm flattered, but there is no way, *ever*, that I will kiss you."

"Of course you'd say that, but I heard you chatting with Dino, telling the dumb racist kid off, and doing many other things. It's too bad I didn't talk to you sooner. I guess it's easier now, since I'm leaving anyway and I won't have to see you everyday knowing you rejected me."

I opened my mouth to say goodnight and leave, when Matteo whispered, "Shhhh!" He wrapped his arm around my shoulders, and pulled me in closer to him and to the perimeter of the bungalow, in the darkest spot.

"Dude, if you're putting the moves on me, I'm gonna kick your *culo*!" I whispered, as he held me close to his chest.

He tried not to chuckle. "It's a patrol… and yes, I *am* putting the moves on you. I thought I had made that clear," he whispered back into my ear.

The kid had a sense of humor. The flashlights of the staff bobbed up and down by the cabins.

I wriggled out of his grasp and Matteo whispered, "I have an idea. Come with me!"

He took my hand and led me away from the patrol. My hand in his made me blush, but I had no time to protest and could not make any noise, so I followed him thinking no one would ever find out. We ran toward the edge of the forest.

Mm, too far.

I removed my hand from Matteo's. "Wait! Where are we going?"

"We're almost there. I wasn't planning on this, but… here, close your eyes." He put his hands on my eyes and guided me forward. The smell of wet leaves and summer melded with the subtle note of Matteo's clean scent. I stumbled, and he caught me. Awkward.

How the hell do I always get myself in the weirdest—

Matteo asked, "Ready?"

"I guess?"

He removed his hands.

Our eyes communicate straight to our brains, but sometimes what we are looking at is so much that our neurons cannot fit it. So they spill it all over our heart, filling it to the brim with wonder and emotions. Mine exploded.

As I opened my eyes, starved from any input, I found myself in a big lawn, nestled among the Tuscan hills, immersed in the biggest swarm of fireflies ever. The little whimsical beings, flickered around us, lighting up the night in a party as magical as private.

"So many!" I exclaimed, in awe.

Matteo chuckled. "You better close your mouth."

I obeyed, thankful I swallowed none of the little creatures. "Wow! How did you find this place?"

He fidgeted looking at his feet. "Well, I could not sleep, lately. It's not the first time I snuck out to come to talk to you… It's just the first time I go through with it."

Wow.

"Matteo, I'm flattered, but there is no way." I turned around to head back to the bungalows, only a few minutes away.

He said, walking at my side. "What if I'm your *soulmate*?"

I laughed. "And a kiss would tell me?"

"I think so. I mean, I'm no expert, but I would

imagine so, and what do you have to lose? What if it's going to be amazing? No one will ever find out, anyway. I leave tomorrow. And I'll talk your ears off, as long as you let me, because if I don't, I'll curse myself for the rest of my days."

He sure had a way with words. And with fireflies. I smiled, and repeated, "No way."

Yet, I sat back on the lawn behind my bungalow and I did let him talk my ears off. For forty-five minutes he spoke into the night about how he'd been dreaming of me, how he wanted nothing more than just one kiss. He wore his feelings like a gorgeous tux. This was no joke. His authenticity illuminated the darkness.

What would have happened if Gio had talked to me without snapping? If he had stuck around to show me what his words had failed to deliver?

Maybe I was so comfortable with Matteo because I had no crush on him, or because he was about my age, or because his declaration had made him vulnerable. He had been so trusting.

"Matteo, I wish I had met you before, but I have to go."

"Leda, now that I talked to you I'm sure you're everything I hoped for and more. Even if I take all night, just one kiss, no tongue, I promise!" He laughed.

I laughed, too. Was he a serial kisser, a player? I asked, "Did you ever kiss anyone?"

Most boys would have answered yes, millions of girls, regardless of the truth, but Matteo just shook his head. My wristwatch read one in the morning.

In that July summer night thick of crickets and breeze, my silence made his hope tangible, like the dew accumulating on the grass stems around us. I wanted to say something but I couldn't, and the space between us became charged with electricity.

Like in a dream I heard myself say, "Okay, but just one kiss, and then we'll never see each other again."

25

Just One Kiss, Dear

Matteo looked thunderstruck. His eyes sparkled in the moonlight, his lips half-closed in amazement, disbelief, and happiness. He hesitated and then got serious. He looked like a man, not a boy.

Despite my skepticism, my heartbeat sped up to an alarming rate. The crickets sang louder, and the sweet smell of wildflowers became more intense.

Matteo closed his eyes and leaned toward me.

I also closed my eyes.

The soft and gentle touch of his lips on mine ignited fireworks inside of me. Everything shook and turned and mixed, merging to detonate in a strong emotion that rose to my blushing face like the foam of a soda bottle, when you open it after shaking it for way too long.

It was a peck, yet I pulled back, stunned, dizzy even. I opened my eyes to see Matteo, as bewildered as I was, staring at me, wide-eyed, for a fraction of a second before I ran away, back to the safety of my bungalow.

What the hell happened?

Wow! Sonia did not lie. If this was what happened with one peck, I could not fathom what making out would be like. I let myself fall into my bed, sighing, face on fire, mind ablaze.

Lisa asked, bleary, "What the hell, Lee? Is that you?"

"No, Lisa, it's Schillaci, go back to sleep."

She sat on her bed. "We were worried sick! What time is it?"

I looked at my wristwatch and answered, "One-thirty, wow."

"What happened?"

And so I told her, still shaken myself, the incredible story of my first kiss. Then I remembered about the wish bracelet I had made only two weeks before, the one supposed to break once I was ready for my first kiss: *stronzate*. I looked at my wrist, and the bracelet was gone.

The next day at breakfast, I threw furtive glances around looking for Matteo's eyes.

Dino asked, "Searching for someone?"

"Um, hi. No?" I lied, studying his unusual aggressive mood.

"Well, that's strange, because a Matteo kid asked me to give you this note this morning at dawn."

"Ah, thank you?" I held out my hand trying to prevent my happiness to show, given Dino's obvious disapproval. I wondered what bit him, but I unfolded the paper instead.

"Dear Leda,

I promised I d disappear from your life, but I can t stop hoping that you ll write soon. I was right!"

The note ended with his signature and address.

Was he my soulmate for real? Dino's scowl brought me back to earth in no time.

Annoyed, I asked, "*What*?"

I wished I could savor my two-seconds of happiness, for once, without a major drama falling my way. He stood up and left, leaving me to wonder what the hell was wrong with him.

On our last night, Lisa, Francesca, and I got ready for the graduation ceremony, the ritual that concluded each week at the *Ciocco Ragazzi*. Since we had witnessed it the week before, we tried to guess what diplomas we might have earned during our stay.

"Miss Slutty Pants!" Francesca said, sticking her tongue out at Lisa.

Lisa protested, "But I didn't even get to make out once!"

Francesca laughed. "But you wished you did, pretty much with anyone!"

Lisa added, "Who would have guessed, Miss Slutty Pants got nothing and Miss Tough Cookie got lucky instead!"

I liked the sound of Miss Tough Cookie; it would have been a perfect summer camp graduation name.

Francesca joked, "More like Miss Midnight Kisser!"

"Wait, wait!" Lisa said, "What about Miss Moonlight Kisser?"

I smiled. "I doubt Dino knows of my wild adventures. He's been acting weird today, right?"

Lisa looked at the frilly top she had laid on her bed. "What do you mean?"

I explained, "Well, he was snippy and then avoided me like the plague."

Francesca said, "All the chemicals in your brain make you see anyone who does *not* serenade you for hours in the moonlight as unfriendly."

I laughed, agreeing it must be nothing, but I still regretted I didn't get to chat with Dino on our last day together, since he had been a good friend. Perhaps he had found out that, lost in my thoughts, I had burned the precious heather stick meant to roast the marshmallows.

Lisa, Francesca, and I sat beside each other, a few rows away from the improvised stage on the grassy hill, waiting to hear our names as Dino called the graduating kids one by one. They stood up and collected their diploma among applause and cheering.

"Riccardo, Diploma of Mr. Explorer!"

"Romina, Diploma of Miss Tree Climber!"

I clapped my hands even if I climbed trees much better than Romina. I swore Dino threw a dagger or two at me as he read her title, too. *Weird.* Lisa received a diploma of Miss Gorgeous and then came the stabbing to my chest.

"Leda, Diploma of Miss Cheater!"

What?

Everyone applauded, unsure. I stood up in a daze, barely noticing Lisa's worried gaze crossing mine. I walked to the stage where Dino didn't look at me, but handed me the freaking piece of paper without shaking my hand and moved on to call the next kid.

What the hell?

Happiness never lasted much. I dragged my heartache and my shame, neatly rolled up in the shape of a diploma tied with a red ribbon, back to my chair.

Lisa put a hand on my knee and said, "Lee, I'm so sorry."

I tried to hold back the tears. "I don't understand what the hell got into him!"

Lisa asked, avoiding my eyes, "Promise not to get mad?"

"*About*?" A terrible foreboding stretched its roots inside of me.

Meanwhile, Dino kept calling kids on stage. "Francesca, Diploma of Miss Comedian!" Francesca rolled her eyes, but smiled as she took her diploma and shook Dino's hand.

Lisa sighed, and confessed, "It's my fault. Dino asked me about Matteo. I told him you were… *together*. Well, I couldn't tell him you were making out with a perfect stranger after curfew, right?"

"You know darn well I wasn't!" I retorted.

"Sorry," she said, lowering her gaze. "I should have minded my own business." I agreed. She added, "How was I to know you had a thing going with Dino, too? I mean you said seventeen was too old! Is it even legal?"

I laughed so loud that I had to cover my face

with my arms.

Leda the seductress, what a joke!

In the general clapping not too many noticed my outburst. Lisa asked, “Have you lost your mind?”

“*You* did! How could you think I had something going with Dino?”

Lisa blushed. “Well, you’re so mature and all, and he got *so* upset!”

“I’m sure it would *not* be legal. *Gross.*” I shuddered.

She laughed, too, breathing more freely now that things were clear, and I wasn’t as angry as she had feared, at least not with *her*. Francesca sat back at Lisa’s other side.

Lisa’s face went from laughter to serious to puzzled. She asked, “Then, what the hell is wrong with him? Why would he call you a cheater?”

I shrugged. “I have no idea, but sure like hell I will find find out.”

He would get a piece of my mind, the jerk.

At the end of the graduation ceremony, I waded against the crowd of kids leaving to go to the clubhouse to play video games. I struggled toward Dino who rushed away. Did he want to avoid me so much that he was running for the hills? I was furious he had shamed me in front of the whole camp but eager to make peace and solve the misunderstanding.

"Dino!" I called.

"I don't wanna talk about it!" he yelled throwing his hands up in the air without looking back.

"Oh, yeah? Well, *I do*! If you didn't wanna talk about *it*, you shouldn't have been a *stronzo* in the first place!"

I couldn't believe I had just said that, and that in spite of myself I was crying. He stopped, turned around and looked at me, his eyes still angry and disappointed. It felt like a whiplash on my wounded soul, but I was determined to clear this ugly mess.

He was twenty-one and much more mature than the rest of us, yet he turned around and yelled back, "Oh, *come on*, Leda! Don't you even try to play the guilty card with me! You cheated!"

"On whom? With whom?" I was so bewildered that he stalled.

"Don't play dumb!" he answered. "You cheated on Stefano with this Matteo guy! I've got my share of cheaters, and there I was, all concerned you might be *lonely*! Lonely *my culo*!"

What? This was about him, not me. *Some*one had cheated on him in the past and he took my business way too personally.

I heard my voice sobbing explanations, "The thing that hurts the most is that you never even asked! Did I tell you that Stefano and I were together? That I even *liked* him? Or that I was with Matteo? Well, I sure didn't, because none of the above ever happened!"

"*What*? But Mara said—and Lisa…"

"I don't freaking care what Lisa and Mara said!" I yelled like Catherine in *Wuthering Heights*.

He frowned. "Why wouldn't you tell *me*? And who the hell is this Matteo?"

"I *tried* to tell you!" I explained. "At the bonfire, but you wouldn't let me speak, and it didn't matter, since I met Matteo only yesterday and well, he's gone, isn't he? But what do you care? Keep your freaking diploma!"

I threw the piece of paper at his bewildered face, turned on my heels and left, still crying. No matter how rightful my claims, he thought me a cheater and a liar, and it hurt like hell. Worse, he did not stop me.

Good thing I was leaving.

The next morning, as I boarded the bus to leave Tuscany, my mood was as awful as when I had left Milan, despite the emotional roller coaster in between.

Like for this entire, crazy, Italian Summer, I thought to myself, recalling the theme song of the lost world cup. Maybe I could blame prepuberty and being hormonal.

A hand clutched my shoulder, and I turned around to say another last minute goodbye. Dino looked sullen as he offered my rolled up diploma.

I looked at the bus. "I don't want it."

"Take it, trust me." His kindness surprised me.

I took the piece of paper, sputtered goodbye and climbed into the bus, curious.

En route to Milan, I unrolled the parchment.

It said, "To Leda, Diploma of Miss Cheater (forgiven)."

Really?

I felt disappointed, betrayed, and even more bitter, because the word *forgiven* implied a crime I had not committed. It implied that Dino was magnanimous, and I was still a cheater.

Son of a puttana. Men suck.

26

Mementos

When the bus approached the sidewalk in Milan, I sought Starry in the crowd. When I saw her, relief soaked me. We hugged tight and loaded the luggage in the car. She took the wheel, and I told her of my adventures, including the kiss and Dino's reaction. She gasped and grimaced, scolding me for letting Matteo talk me into kissing, but I had no regrets.

I asked, "And how was your vacation with the Soldanti?" I always called her boyfriend by his last name to increase the distance between me and him.

"We went to Burma, it was amazing."

"Where?"

"In Southeast Asia. They just changed the name

of the country to Myanmar."

She told me about the places she had visited, the culture, and the food, but she did not mention the Soldanti.

I asked, "Is everything all right with the Soldanti?"

"Same old. Ups and down."

She changed the topic as we pulled into our driveway. She parked in the garage, and I ran into the house.

My sister Viola was watching TV in the living room. She steered away her gaze from Video Music and asked, "Hey, Kiddo, how was summer camp?"

"Awesome!"

She looked amused, "Oh yeah? Did you get anything going? Because I've heard of some funny business with a seventeen-year-old."

I blushed. "Well, yeah, no. Nothing happened, but you know Starry…"

She rolled her eyes. "I sure do. She's still upset about Easter."

"Easter?"

"She didn't tell you? I ran off to Germany to see Volker." She had been dating her German boyfriend for over a year now.

"Wow, no wonder she's still upset."

"It was worth it." Viola winked as Starry called us to eat a dinner of cereal and milk.

Sometimes I wished Mom could cook. But then again, if I had a wish I'd make love last forever like in the books and the movies, like in *The Princess Bride*.

Yet, Viola had ditched Renzo, I had been mulling over my feelings for Nico for years before falling head over heels for Gio and kissing a perfect stranger.

So much for a *nun*, Nico!

Even my parents had split. I thought of the boys populating my summer. They didn't know *me*, the *real* me. Nico did. Unfortunately I would not see him for several weeks and then… Were we even going to be in speaking terms?

For now I had only one night to say hi to my friends in Arese before leaving for the seaside with Dad and Viola.

After dinner I ran to call Sonia.

Her mother opened the door. "Hi Leda, Sonia is already out."

Disappointment radiated through me. Had she forgotten that I was coming back? I walked to the tennis courts. Gio was nowhere in sight. A lot of friends were on vacation with their families. Sonia was sitting on the sidewalk by Martino, chatting.

"Look who's here!" Alex yelled, running to give

me a power hug.

"Yo, Alex!" A tan made him even more handsome than I remembered. Sonia pried him off me and sequestered me in a corner.

I asked, "How goes it, girlfriend? You seem happy." I nodded toward Martino who was laughing with the older guys. Sonia blushed, looking at the asphalt. A first. I prodded, "So, is it official? Do you like Martino?"

She fidgeted. "Ah, nooo, of course not, I mean, he's ten!" She looked at her hands and her lips trembled. "Okay, I do, but I don't know what to do about it."

"You said he's mature, and if you like him, go for it, right?"

Sonia sighed. "And he's a great kisser."

I almost rolled my eyes at her shallowness before remembering my own recent sins. I swallowed. "Ah, yeah. That too."

Sonia quirked an eyebrow. "No sermon? Lee, you've changed. What happened to you?"

I caught her up, and her eyes almost fell out of her sockets. "WHAT? You turned down the man of your dreams and kissed a random guy? What is wrong with you?"

I shrugged. Just because I was smart *most of the time* it didn't mean that my actions had to always make sense. "Gee, Sonia, I don't know! Gio terrified me, and when I tried to say so he got angry and scarier! Instead, when I rejected Matteo he spent the whole night talking to me, like there was no other place he'd rather be. That's why I kissed him, I guess. Does that make sense?"

Sonia rolled her eyes, huffing. "No, but you never do."

"Whatever. I've got to go already. Are you leaving for the seaside, too?"

Sonia nodded, smirking. "I'll be in Ostia, forcing myself on Ermanno. Remember the one who doesn't know I'm his girlfriend? At least he's older than me." Sonia giggled, then stood up to hug me.

I also stood. "You behave, girl. Do nothing I wouldn't do."

Sonia broke in a mischievous grin. "Like kissing random people?"

"Shhhhh!" I punched her arm.

"I'll see you in September, Lee. Be well!"

"You too." I hugged her back. "Goodnight everyone! Have a good summer!" I yelled to the crowd.

"Bye, Lee! Send postcards! See you in September!" they yelled back.

Meanwhile Alex walked up to us, Francesco at his side, and said, "Man! Sonia used up your time. May we walk you home?" He offered his arm in a gallant gesture.

"Sure, dude, but you forget whom you're speaking to," I answered, ignoring his arm, hoping my tough kid attitude masked how flattered I felt. Francesco snickered walking beside me, but Alex stopped.

"*Dude*? I'm the *great* Alex. And *whom* would I be speaking to?"

"Someone who doesn't care for your Mom-entrancing tricks, *dude*," I smiled.

Alex and Francesco walked beside me. The night was muggy, the thick air lacerated by a cicada.

Alex smirked. "Oh, yeah. I almost forgot, you act more like trucker than a girl. My bad. How was your vacation?"

I tried to ignore his charming smile, cursing the effect of hormones on my brain, turning my friends into *males.*

How did I not notice before?

Alex repeated, "Hello? Miss Trucker? Your vacation?"

"Wait, who's a *Miss* now?"

Francesco laughed out loud. "I can't believe you're upset about the Miss and not the *trucker* part."

I answered, "There's nothing wrong with truckers."

"They swear a lot," Francesco pointed out.

"So do I," I teased.

"True story," Francesco confirmed.

"Mr. Trucker it is," Alex conceded. "Now, can you tell us about your vacation?"

I loved friends who cared about how my vacation was, who wanted to walk me home, and found my lame jokes at least mildly entertaining. The fact that Alex was easy on the eyes, I decided, could only be a perk.

This was turning out to be the best summer of my life. Italy didn't win the world cup (and to Klara's elation, Volker's, and mine, Germany had kicked Maradona's *culo* in the final) but at least I had found friends who didn't mind too much that I was a girl, and a weird one at that.

My seaside vacation passed in a blur, ending with a gradual and shocking realization I was not looking forward to share with Starry. Vera, Dad's friend who had rescued me from our disastrous car accident on our way to Bormio, was in fact Dad's GIRLfriend. I liked her a lot better than the Soldanti.

It was the second day of September and Mom picked me up in Milan, on the way back from her own vacation. She hugged me, but the curve of her shoulders held a heaviness reflected in the wrinkles of her tanned face.

"Is everything okay?" I asked.

She shrugged. "We can't move to Milan. It's too expensive."

I tried not to beam at her when I said, "Sorry."

Yet, I couldn't shake the feeling there might have been something else bothering her.

When we pulled in Arese, the enormous poplar in our front yard looked magnificent in the late afternoon golden light. The sound of the *Panda* car crunching the few fallen leaves sounded familiar: soothing and melancholic at the same time. Summer was over, again. It had been a memorable one.

I hopped out of the car and called, "Fuzzeeeeer! Fuzzeeeer!"

The fat cat wobbled down the slope from the backyard, meowing as I opened the mailbox stuffed with postcards from Sonia, Klara, Alex… One fell to the ground and I leaned down to get it, exchanging purring effusions with Fuzzer, rubbing against my leg.

Wait a second…

The postcard on the ground came from Sicily.

Is it possible that…?

Starry gasped, and I snatched my head up.

"Starry, what's wrong?" I asked.

She was standing in front of a pile of random stuff on our doorstep and didn't answer. I reached her with the mail in my hands. Her eyes were open wide, and her mouth was frozen in a grimace of distaste as if she had just swallowed cough syrup. She approached the haphazard collection of goods, tears welling into her eyes and I panicked.

What the cazzo?

Mom turned teary-eyed as she stared at the random pile of stuff on our stoop: a plant, clothes, some boxes.

"Starry, *what*? Are you all right?"

"Yeah, yeah. Everything's fine," she answered, swallowing hard.

"Fine *col cazzo*! What's *wrong*? I'm not five anymore; you can talk to me!"

She didn't even yell at me for my language. She approached the pile in a haze, lifting a t-shirt from a box, touching the leaves of the plant.

I prodded, "*So?*"

"It's Marco. We broke up. I guess you were right. He *was* a *stronzo*."

"*What?* He sure was!" I put my arm around her tiny self.

When Starry had told me I didn't like him because I was jealous, I had trusted her growing psychologist's wisdom. I had assumed that grown-ups were right. Now I knew better. I was becoming an adult myself, not because I was right, but because I mistrusted everybody else.

I hugged Starry, relieved she had gotten rid of her obnoxious boyfriend but sorry about her broken heart. I should have guessed it. She didn't mention him at all after the Burma vacation.

I asked, puzzled, "What's with all the gifts, then?"

"This is all the stuff I ever gave to him. I guess he returned it, leaving it here, who knows for how long."

Nobody had been at the house in a while, except the handyman who fed Fuzzer, since Viola was back to Padua to study for her fall session. After surviving high school she had become a stellar student in college.

I helped Starry to carry everything inside. "Should we throw this stuff away? Donate it?"

"Nah. I mean, I bought it because I liked it," Starry replied.

I nodded, bringing another box in the foyer.

It's fascinating how we keep mementos of our most humiliating and sad moments, dragging them along for years. The cheater diploma was rolled up on my shelf beside my ski cups and the bronze medal I had won for third place in a swimming competition with three participants on my eleventh birthday.

Was it the way we were raised? I had spent my childhood looking at the cross where we nailed the son of God. Why wouldn't we remember him while multiplying the bread and fish, or while curing the leper? Perhaps to remind ourselves of how epically we had fucked up, to be humble, to never make the same errors.

I touched the shriveling leaves of the abandoned plant. "This could be pretty if it recovered. What is it?"

"It's a *ficus benjamina*."

"*Ben*, got it."

I dropped the small plant, Ben, into the living room by a window. It would become an integral part of our life, another monument to capital mistakes. Too often our little mementos turn into a huge ballast of guilt and fear, freezing us into the inability to do nothing but hang on to our failures for dear life. We whine and blame them, avoiding to take responsibility for our own unhappiness.

Starry was sorting through the boxes, muttering to herself.

I asked, "Do you want me to stick around?"

"No, Lee, thank you. Go out with your friends. We broke up weeks ago. It's just the shock of finding this stuff."

I nodded and dragged our luggage upstairs, mail under my arm. As soon as I reached my bedroom, I dropped the suitcases and searched for the postcard from Sicily in the midst of the colorful pile. It was a sunset on Siracusa, the magnificent pastel-colored buildings reflected on the still waters of the *lungomare*. I turned it around. In a familiar tiny writing, all scraggly corners, it read,

"Hi Lee,

I hope you're having a great summer.

Nico"

Holy cow!

My knees gave in and I plopped on the bed, hugging the postcard to my chest, lava rising to my head.

Nico wrote me a postcard! Nico the Thug!

It meant nothing, but I slid the card in the back pocket of my jeans, and I left for the pool to catch up with my friends.

27

Out of the Nest

I trotted into the pool grounds and yelled, “Soniaaa! Soniaaa!”

I spotted her and a few others under the portico of the little clubhouse sitting on the grassy mound beside the water.

“Leeee!” my friend screeched, running toward me and lifting me in a huge hug. She was even taller than I remembered.

When she put me down, I waved. “Hi everyone!”

Martino smiled and nodded from afar. Alex and Francesco walked closer to say hi, and Alex engulfed me in a power hug. He seemed… older, more manly, and I found myself not knowing where to put my hands when I hugged him back.

“Where’s everyone else?” I asked, pulling away

and looking at the grass.

I sure hope I'm not freaking blushing. That postcard melted my brain.

"Gio hasn't been around much," Sonia answered.

I hated her bluntness more than usual since Alex and Francesco were part of the conversation.

"Who cares!" I lied. "I mean Valerio, Oli, Klara…"

Sonia pointed at the water. "They're all there. We came to chill in the shade. Laura is on vacation still."

Alex chimed in, "How was your summer?"

Sonia pushed him away. "None of this nonsense! I need Lee to myself." She clutched my wrist and dragged me to the swings, just like old times. I felt relieved to increase the distance between me and Alex, who looked like he had been working out all summer.

Or maybe my brain shrunk.

As we sat in the golden light of the ripening afternoon, Sonia blurted, "Oh my God, Lee, I'm *in love*!"

"What's new…" I smiled, forcing an eye roll.

"No, Dummy! *For real*!" Sonia was beaming, her green eyes bright like emeralds in her face flushed by the sun.

"Tell me everything."

"So, I went to Ostia, like every summer.

Remember Ermanno?"

I smirked. "Yeah, the boyfriend who didn't know you were his girlfriend."

"Exactly! I was on a mission to change my status to official girlfriend."

"I guess it worked?"

"Wait! I pulled out all my best moves, sideway glances, groping, rubbing, giggling, the whole repertoire. On *Ferragosto* he was drunk and could not resist me."

I laughed. "Don't tell me you raped Ermanno!"

"I mean, we only kissed."

"Dummy, I was joking. How was it?"

Sonia answered, "Meh. Nothing compared to Martino's kiss."

"No way!"

"Yes way!"

"That kid's a phenomenon."

Sonia smiled, googly eyed. "He sure is."

"Nooooo!" This was going somewhere I did not expect.

"Yes! Ermanno later said he was drunk and *didn't mean to* make out." Sonia gagged. "Such a cod. Forget him! As soon as I came back to Arese, I smiled to Martino and dangled my hand close to his. He didn't flinch as if he had known all along." She sighed holding her chest with her hands, rocking on the swing. "He took my hand and kissed me, just like that. The most amazing kiss ever."

"*No shit*! Better than the epic forsythia make out session?"

Sonia nodded. "We've been together since. I'm living the dream. I want nothing more."

"Wow, that's awesome! He does look so mature…"

"He is. With being adopted and all, he put up with some rough stuff…"

"He *what*?"

Sonia quirked an eyebrow. "I mean, I hadn't realized that either, but Tino and Valerio are black. No way they were born here."

Italians ranged from white to dark, but the two brothers' gorgeous brown did not look indigenous.

I shrugged. "It makes sense. Does everyone know?"

Sonia sighed, a silly smile lightening up her tanned face. "At first we kept it quiet, but then we held hands in public, stuff like that. No one said anything. I guess we're sooo cute together that the age difference doesn't matter."

I pictured them in my mind: Sonia was at least twenty centimeters taller than Martino.

"Yeah," I said. "You two are *adorable*, except that you look like his mom."

"Oh, shut it! Beauty is in the eye of the beholder," Sonia quoted.

Wow, who's the Lolita, after all?

I had been so quick in judging my friend, when

instead she had fallen for a ten-year-old, scrawny kid and was justifying her love by an educated quote. Me? I thought I was smart and mature, yet in spite of my ancient feelings for Nico, I had broken the heart of the old hunk I had fallen head over heels for and kissed a perfect stranger. Way to go, Leda!

Sonia asked, "*What*?"

"Ah, no, nothing. It's just that… Where did you get that quote from?"

"*Cioé*. We've been dating for a week, already! Isn't that great?"

"Wow! That's your record!"

We hopped off the swings and walked back to the others. Sonia's eyes were on Tino, ahead of us beside Alex, Francesco, Klara, and Oli. The sunlight tinged the dry grass almost orange, same as Alex's golden hair, messier and… sexier than ever?

Oh, my.

I sighed.

Nico was right, puberty is a mess. Hormones muddled my brain.

I sighed again, touching the back pocket of my jeans, rigid with the postcard.

Nico, the constant in my life, the perfect match for Mr. Hyde.

The sun was warmer on my cheeks.

As I joined my friends, a new resolution took root

within me. I would sweep Nico off his freaking thug's feet. I clenched my fists. After all my mistakes, at least I was braver. The middle of my world had shifted from my home to a place I didn't know yet, somewhere *out of the nest.*

I can do this!

I didn't want to be late for dinner so, as Sonia settled on Tino's scrawny knees, I yelled, "See ya later!"

Alex trotted up to me. "Lee, can I walk you home? I need to talk to you."

Holy mother of Jesus. "Ah, sure, man. What's ailing you this time?" I asked, walking toward the gate.

"Ailing?" Alex chuckled. "I missed you!"

"Whatever! So, what's up?"

"Pretty deep stuff, as usual."

I looked away from his hazel eyes, similar to Matteo's. A little shiver ran down my spine at the memory of my unforgettable first kiss.

The silence grew heavy, so I prodded him. "A-hem. Pretty deep *merda*, you said?"

"I said *stuff*."

I laughed. "Right, your rigid upbringing would never allow you to swear like *a trucker.*"

He laughed, too. "Oh yeah, I forgot, dear Mr. Trucker."

"Right. You're Mr. *Sucker*, instead."

"I'm not sure *sucker* qualifies as trucker language."

"You still are."

More silence. I kicked a pebble. We were walking along the same old sidewalk I recognized crack by crack. The same moss growing in the shady spots, the sweet scents of summer drenching the humid evening but with less jasmine and with a hint of dried leaves instead. Yet, everything was different, less overwhelming… at least if I ignored how Alex's t-shirt clung to his shoulders.

He said, "So! I'm the biggest fool on earth."

"Sounds right," I answered way too fast, relieved to express how much I did *not* like him.

He poked my side but without the usual malice. "I … thought I liked Sonia, but all she wanted was to make out."

"Are you *complaining*?" I chuckled. This was not boy behavior and something was really wrong with him.

"Well, yes. I felt lonely. And making out wasn't that great, you know?"

"Yeah," I lied, since I had never made out, and the one kiss of my life had been mind blowing.

"You don't," Alex stated.

"*What*?"

He smirked. "You've never made out."

"We were talking about *you*," I reminded him, frowning.

"Right, I had assumed that you and Gio… Anyway, it doesn't matter. Long story short. I was barking up the wrong tree."

I saw where this was going; Alex needed advice on a girl. I couldn't believe he needed any. He mussed his wild golden hair, shutting his eyes, and I stared too long.

He resumed, "I want a girlfriend I can talk to. Someone smart. Someone I care about."

"*A-men*! I agree. A pretty face might send your head reeling, but if you can't talk to the person, it's a waste of time."

Could I talk to Nico? The few times we had spoken we had fought.

Alex interrupted my train of thought, "Right! Doesn't it make sense?"

"It sure does, Man. So what's your dilemma?"

As I stared at his face, I understood the question he had not dared to ask.

He glued his gaze on me, a slight blush betraying feelings I had not suspected one minute before. My lips parted in the biggest surprise of that wondrous summer of 1990. Alex was so darn handsome. His wild hair made him seem like the rebel he pretended to be. Instead, he was sweet and sincere even if he had done questionable deeds. Boys will be boys. He could be a jerk. His mesmerizing eyes, locked on mine, held no promise of that. My catatonic state was interrupted by his question.

"Lee, do you want to be my girlfriend?"

I swallowed hard, feeling Nico's postcard heavy

in the back pocket of my jeans. Nico had thought of *me*! But did that mean anything? The chance that Nico the Thug had a heart, and that maybe, in one of the least dark corners, he even liked me a little was slim.

Alex instead was standing right in front of me, handsome as ever and interested. Could I turn down the perfect boy for a non-existent chance at an impossible love with the kid version of the antichrist?

END OF BOOK 2

The whole Italian Saga and many more books by Gaia B Amman are available on Amazon or can be ordered from your favorite bookstore.

Get the latest news, say hi, register for the monthly newsletter, and learn more about Italy and its customs at: www.gaiabamman.com

About Gaia B Amman

Photo credit @BethInsalaco

Gaia B. Amman was born and raised in Italy. She moved to the United States in her twenties to pursue her Ph.D. in molecular biology. She's currently a professor of biology at D'Youville College in Buffalo, New York, where she was voted "the professor of the month" by her students. Her research and commentaries have been published in prestigious, international, peer-reviewed journals, including *Nature*.

A bookworm from birth, she wrote throughout her childhood and won two short story competitions in Italy in her teens. Gaia is an avid traveler, and many of her adventures are an inspiration for her fiction. Mostly she is passionate about people and the struggles they face to embrace life. Her highest hope is to reach and help as many as she can through her writing and her teaching. She authored the *Indie Author Guide*, the LGBTQ sci-fi fantasy *Linked—Will Empathy Save the United Terrestrial Democracy?*, *The Italian Saga*, a Middle Grade/YA four-novel series of which you just read the second volume, and the *Sonder Series*, which follows Leda's adventures in college and as a new adult. The books, light-hearted and funny at first sight, deal with issues like sexuality, divorce, friendship, abuse, human rights, gender stereotypes, first love, and self-discovery.

Among Amman's favorite authors are J.K. Rowling, Jandy Nelson, Neil Gaiman, Chuck Palahniuk, Kurt Vonnegut, J.R.R. Tolkien, and Antoine de Saint Exupèry.

For book updates follow the blog at www.gaiabamman.com and subscribe to the newsletter.

More books by GB Amman:

Following Leda's Adventures:
The Italian Saga (4 novels, YA)

Sonder Series (Women's Literature, Contemporary)

Others:

Romance Fantasy, Sci-Fi

Acknowledgements

Many thanks to all the people who supported me through this crazy endeavor: Seth Amman for his unconditional love, Amy Joslyn, who read and reread the books doling precious advice, Paul Schwartzmeyer for sharing his experience and knowledge, Marina Bozzi, Valeria Bistulfi, and Silvia Paesante for reading and loving (me more than the books), Pat Obermeier, Neil Daniel, Joel Inbody, Sarah DiThomas, Mari Lee Kozlowski, Linda Tryzna, Gary Friedman, Sabrina Poena Young, Michael Kelley, Agatha Berger, and Gary Earl Ross for their critique, Carol Amman for proofing, Mark Amman for help with anything technical, Patrick Finan and Brandon Davis for their advice on media and marketing, César Cedano, Ed Stehlik, and Rodney Garrison for being the best friends anyone could ever want, my dad for being his awesome, supportive self, Mattia Licastro for being my kid best friend and for sharing his video games, D'Youville College for helping people become the best they can be, the Tumblr community, Scriggler, and You, who read this book all the way through the acknowledgments:

THANK YOU, from the bottom of my heart.

— Gaia B. Amman

Discussion questions

- Leda mentions a few women she uses as a role model. Who are they? Why, in your opinion, doesn't she compare herself to Starry?
- Leda mentions several times she would like to be a male. Do you think her wish is genuine or dictated by cultural circumstances? What triggers this reaction in chapter three? And in chapter thirteen? Did you ever wish you were a member of the opposite sex? Why yes or no?
- What was the idea of women in Italy in 1990, at least as perceived by Leda through television? (See chapter two.)
- Which one of Lee's teachers do you think is really bad? Which one is just giving her "tough love"? What was or is your experience with your own teachers?
- Italy is often perceived like a very religious (Catholic) country. Can you remember any

religious references throughout the book? What are some positive aspects of religion in Lee's life? And some negative ones?

- Do you recall any instances in the book in which religion becomes entangled with superstition and tradition?
- How do Leda's prayers evolve from the beginning to the end of the book?
- How did Sonia's character evolve throughout the book, at lcast in Leda's eyes?
- Are there any characters of color in the story? Who are they? Based on Lee's comments and her experience, was it a big deal to be of color in Italy in 1990? Why do you think is that?
- Do you recall any instance of racism in the book? Toward whom? Why do you think is that? Why, do you think, people are racist?
- Did you learn about any singular Italian traditions? Do you recall what Saint Fermin is about?
- Why does Starry want to move to Milan? Does Lee want to move? Why? Who's right, in your opinion?
- How do you feel about menstruation? When did you learn about it? How? Did your perception of this natural phenomenon change with time?
- There are several descriptions of Italian

landscapes throughout the book. Which was your favorite? Why?

- How does Gio reacts to Lee's rejection? And Matteo? What are the consequences of their reactions?
- Why, in your opinion, is Dino so mean to Lee? Think about someone who made you really mad recently. Is it possible that you reacted so strongly to their behavior because of your personal history?
- How does the relationship between Starry and Leda evolve?
- Does Starry behave more like a mom or like a friend in your opinion?
- Do you know any teen magazine similar to the Italian *Cioè*? Did you ever read them? Were they helpful in any way?
- What's your impression of soccer fans in Italy? Was the world cup a big deal? Do you have a similar experience about a sport in your country?
- Leda and her friends seem very concerned about the way they look. Why is that in your opinion? Did you feel the same way growing up, regardless of your sex?
- How does the relationships with our parents affect who we are? For example, think about Leda, Nico, and Baccellati (the lanky kid who did not swim to guard the flip-flops).

From the little you know about their parents, does their behavior make sense?

- What do you think of the relationship between Sonia and Leda? Did you ever have a tight friendship with someone whose behavior was very different from yours?
- What do you think Leda will answer to Alex's question at the end the book? What would you answer?

60659607R10192

Made in the USA
San Bernardino, CA
12 December 2017